A Candlelight Ecstasy Romance™

"... OR MAYBE YOU'RE TELLING ME THAT YOUR FAVORS ARE PRICELESS."

With a quick movement he encircled her hips and pulled her against him. He lowered his mouth to hers again. Captured there, helpless to escape, Wynn felt his heat through the gauzy chiffon of her dress. As Aaron's lips left her mouth to nuzzle the sensitive spot where her ear lobe met her cheek, Wynn shivered against him. His breath hot in her ear, he whispered huskily, "You're right to hold yourself so dear, little bride, if this is a fair sample of your wares."

A TOUCH OF HEAVEN

Tess Holloway

A CANDLELIGHT ECSTASY ROMANCE™

Published by
Dell Publishing Co., Inc.
1 Dag Hammarskjold Plaza
New York, New York 10017

ISBN: 0-440-18931-4

Printed in the United States of America
First printing—December 1982

To Our Readers:

We have been delighted with your enthusiastic response to Candlelight Ecstasy Romances™, and we thank you for the interest you have shown in this exciting series.

In the upcoming months we will continue to present the distinctive sensuous love stories you have come to expect only from Ecstasy. We look forward to bringing you many more books from your favorite authors and also the very finest work from new authors of contemporary romantic fiction.

As always, we are striving to present the unique, absorbing love stories that you enjoy most—books that are more than ordinary romance.

Your suggestions and comments are always welcome. Please write to us at the address below.

Sincerely,

The Editors
Candlelight Romances
1 Dag Hammarskjold Plaza
New York, New York 10017

*To my darling daughters,
Jan, Lisa, Erica, and Amy—
four little women who have grown up
in the most delightful ways*

A TOUCH OF HEAVEN

CHAPTER ONE

Wynn Harris wondered whose wife she'd be tonight. As her coltish legs covered the two blocks between the bus stop and the office building, she breathed deeply of the moist, tangy sea breeze blowing in from San Francisco Bay. Amazingly there was no fog, but the early morning chill of this August day made her glad of her gray flannel slacks and the navy blue blazer she wore over her white silk blouse.

A gentle remembering smile curved her full pink lips as she thought of the gentleman whose wife she'd been last night. Wynn hoped the last four Friday evenings had been as pleasant and relaxing for Professor Jenkins as they'd been for her, sitting by the fire in his elegant study on Russian Hill, she sipping herb tea, he sipping Napoleon brandy, while she read to him from *Madame Bovary*. In fact, Wynn enjoyed this assignment so much that last night, once again, she'd stayed beyond the agreed-upon time to finish the chapter in which Emma Bovary's romantic fancies and illusions are cruelly destroyed by a letter of renunciation and betrayal from her caddish lover.

When Wynn closed the book with a sad smile, the professor sighed. "You read so beautifully; I'll be quite sorry when my eye infection clears up, Wynn." Gazing intently at her face, he added thoughtfully, "You know, it's odd how much you resemble Emma Bovary as Flaubert describes her, with your hair parted in the center and

11

pulled back like two black wings into a chignon and your fine eyes so brown they seem black under those heavy lashes. . . ."

Holding up a soft well-formed hand, Wynn laughingly protested. "Please, Professor, stop! It's only by chance that I'm wearing my hair this way tonight. I don't want to be compared too closely to poor Emma. I don't want my life to end in tragedy as hers did!"

A smile on his thin, ascetic face, the professor shook his iron-gray head. "No chance of that with you, Wynn. You're not like most young women of your generation. They'd completely approve of poor Emma's restlessness. They'd think her absolutely right to despise her life and detest being the wife of an ordinary country doctor. Few of them would see beneath the surface to the shallowness and futility of her yearnings for a life of sensation and glitter."

Wynn murmured, "It's so sad. I know Emma's husband was a dull and plodding fellow, but if only she'd been capable of recognizing the value of his devotion."

When Wynn arose to leave, the professor saw her to the door. "Thank heavens you aren't one of those faddish young women who scorn traditional family life and want to be race-car drivers or fork-lift operators instead!"

Wynn laughed in mild admonishment. "Now, Professor, you mustn't let living in San Francisco fool you into thinking that there aren't still hundreds of thousands of young women who want above all to marry a good man and raise a family. I'm not such a rarity. I just seem to be because we live in a city that strains against all the old boundaries."

"Rarity or not," Roger Jenkins replied, "you're a gem, Wynn, and I sometimes fear that in this day and age, there isn't a man alive under forty who's worthy of you."

Now Wynn swung along at the city's quick but not hectic pace, thinking ruefully of Professor Jenkins's words last night. She had no doubt that there were plenty of men "worthy" of her. After all, there was nothing special about her, she knew. But sometimes, lately, her hopes flagged that she'd ever meet a man she could love in that special way that would last forever and a day.

Yes, Wynn met plenty of men, especially in her line of work. Take Ed, for instance. Perhaps Ed was even The One and she was too blind and foolish to see it, Wynn considered as she wound her way through the crowds. She did sort of love Ed, she thought, in a way. A very quiet way. He was a good man, a kind and thoughtful man. And she had ample evidence that he cared for her very much. And yet kissing him was like eating vanilla pudding: all right once in a while, but too bland for every day.

Wynn laughed aloud at her thought, causing a passerby to glance at her nervously. Not that she wanted a daily diet of hot pepperoni pizza either. No, thank you! she thought sardonically. Wynn's own mother's experience with the zesty, hot-blooded type had taught Wynn the dangers of that.

But was it too much to ask that she find a man who was both willing to be a good husband and father and who also was virile, exciting, and fascinating? Wynn frowned. Probably it *was* too much to ask. Well, then she was doomed to a lonely single life because she refused to settle for less.

With a half block to go, Wynn now passed that most wonderful of stores, Domestica. She lingered as she did most mornings to gaze for a few seconds at the window display of the perfect baby's room. She was particularly charmed by the matching wallpaper and curtains, with their smiling clowns floating in a blue sky, held aloft by a gay bunch of balloons in tender pastels of pink, yellow, and green. The color scheme seemed to promise a loving welcome to an infant of either sex—just as Wynn herself would, when and if that joyous day ever came. She spent a few seconds more admiring the sparkling white wicker

13

cradle in the middle of the display. It would be terrible to dust, but so beautiful.

As she reluctantly turned from the window into the pedestrian traffic flow she was bumped from behind by a young man dressed in banker's gray and nudged from the front by a ragged street musician rushing toward his day's post on Union Square, jauntily carrying his flute on his shoulder like a rifle. Glancing at the sensible Timex on her wrist, Wynn quickened her steps. Lula was annoyed when her wives were late to work.

The mica embedded in the concrete in front of Wynn's office building glistened as she passed through the heavy plate glass doors into the starkly elegant modern lobby. The brushed steel elevator doors whispered open. Wynn stepped in and touched a round, flat button. A not unpleasant sensation of falling lifted her stomach as the noiseless elevator rushed to a stop and opened its doors to the travertine walls and parquet floors of the eighth floor.

Wynn pushed open the gleaming rosewood door discreetly marked only Suite 850 and entered the premises of Helpmates, Inc. It was like stepping into a country kitchen of an earlier century. Wynn inhaled with pleasure the homey aromas of baking bread, crisp bacon, and maple syrup—even though she knew they came from sophisticated chemicals diffused into the air through the duct system. The tall, sleek windows of the modern building were transformed by wooden shutters that covered the bottom half while the clear California light poured in through the top half, softened by ruffled brown-and-white gingham curtains. Along the wall facing the office door were pine cabinets that housed the business's files and supplies. Beneath the cabinets an enormous black woodburning stove and an oak icebox stood side by side.

At the far end of the room an old round oak table and chairs stood in the middle of a large oval braided rag rug in shades of brown, burnt orange, black, and beige. Here were held the morning meetings and conferences with clients. Wynn saw that a group of "wives" were already gathered around the table with the usual coffee and sweet rolls, waiting for Lula to arrive and give them their day's assignments.

From behind the large rectangular pine worktable that served as the reception desk, Sherri, the young girl Friday, chirped a cheery hello. "There you are! I'm glad you got here before the boss. She was on the warpath last night when she left."

"What's wrong now? Money troubles again?" Wynn asked with a commiserating smile. Lula Dobbs was a loveable and appealing woman, but her volatile and blustery moods sometimes made life trying for her employees.

Sherri shrugged. "I don't know, but something's sure been bugging her lately." Her voice dropped to a confidential whisper. "You should've heard her hassle Jack yesterday, and you know he's one of her favorite wives."

As Wynn pulled out a chair to join her colleagues' circle, she wondered if Lula's current trouble was personal or business. She knew that Lula's granddaughter was giving her grief lately. Instead of finishing up her last year at Stanford she wanted to drop out of school and marry a young man who Lula felt had no prospects whatever. On the other hand, Helpmates, Inc., still an infant enterprise barely a year old, was often a source of anxiety to its founder.

As Wynn poured herself a cup of coffee she tuned in to the discussion. Jack Clancey was saying, "And I told Lula, 'I'm not about to scrub a kitchen floor as big as a landing field on my hands and knees. This isn't the Middle Ages,' I said. And I bought the scrubber at a discount store; it didn't even cost that much. 'The business can always use an electric floor scrubber,' I told her. 'Think

15

of it as an investment,' I said. But no. She said if I didn't cut down on my expenses she'd either take them out of my wages or fire me.''

Marie, a motherly, unflappable middle-aged woman who'd worked at Helpmates, Inc., as long as Wynn, said to Jack with a teasing smile, "Now, Jack, you know Lula won't fire you. She dotes on you. And, for that matter, so does your client. Why didn't you ask Dr. Kenyon to buy you the scrubber? I'll bet she'd buy you anything you asked for just to keep you happy.''

The others all chimed in with friendly jibes. "I'll say she would." "You can say that again!" Jack had landed a regular cleaning job with a busy single woman doctor who prized his efficient and meticulous work above rubies and diamonds, and it was a continual source of amusement to all the wives that the doctor seemed a bit smitten with Jack's healthy, blond good looks as well.

Jack blushed faintly and laughed. "Come on, you guys, Dr. Kenyon knows our motto: We can give you anything but love.''

As the others all laughed at their in joke, Jack continued. "But I think I will ask her to buy me a new vacuum cleaner. That thing she's got is so old it couldn't suck up thistledown from a pane of glass.''

Then Paul, the only other male wife, and the group's only political activist, said in his fussy, aggrieved tone, "Isn't that just typical? It's always the workers who're expected to make do with inferior equipment while the bosses spare no expense for every faddish gimmick that comes along to make *their* lives easier.''

"What's this about bosses?" a hearty voice called out from the other end of the room. The wives all turned to greet Lula Dobbs, who strode toward them with a smile on her face as bright as the helmet of silver hair on her head. Wynn was relieved to see, by Lula's smile, that whatever had bothered her last night had abated, at least for the time being.

While Lula sat down heavily with a sigh, Wynn patted Paul on the hand and explained, "Paul was about to deliver his lecture on the downtrodden working class and the exploitative managerial class, but your arrival saved us."

Everyone including Paul laughed. He smiled at Lula with real affection as he doffed an imaginary hat to her. "Present company excepted, of course."

"I should think so!" Lula replied. "Especially considering the expense accounts that certain people turn in and expect me to pay," she added, glancing slyly at Jack.

Then amid jokes and laughter the morning assignment meeting began. It was Lula's routine to inform the wives of the work requests that had come in since the last meeting, and through an untidy but mysteriously efficient combination of democracy, tyranny, and anarchy, skills were matched to jobs, personal preferences taken into consideration, and decisions made on who would do which jobs when.

The polishing of a flatware service for twelve was accepted by Paul. "I can do it this afternoon and she'd better supply me with decent silver paste," he said ominously, "or I'll bring my own and put it on her bill."

Before Wynn could volunteer, Marie claimed an open-ended assignment for ten to twelve every morning to lavish attention and affection on a two-year-old boy whose feelings were sorely trampled by the arrival of a newborn baby sister in his house.

Jack's assignment, set for next Wednesday afternoon at four, was to do his famous magic routine for a little girl's eighth birthday party. Paul offered to go along as photographer at no cost but materials, just for the fun of it.

Lula held up the last three-by-five card between her long-nailed, red-laquered fingertips. "This one is a bit out of the ordinary," she said thoughtfully. "Let me read it to

17

you just as I took it down from the client's secretary, word for word: Gentleman of means requires young woman, under thirty, to accompany him to a business dinner at the restaurant, Le Bourgogne, as his wife. The applicant must be of good background and must possess beauty of a quiet, elegant, and classical type."

As one, every face turned to gaze at Wynn, then turned back to Lula. Marie spoke up with a note of disapproval in her voice. "I wouldn't want Wynn to walk into a messy situation. It sounds as if they think this is an escort service."

"Exactly what I thought," Lula agreed. "And I explained to the secretary that we weren't. But she said the gentleman understood that we supplied any service a wife might render except, of course, conjugal services. It seems that in this particular business meeting, it's important that the client appear to be married."

Paul said darkly, "You be careful, Wynn. It sounds exploitative to me."

"Why does everyone assume *I'll* take this job?" Wynn protested. "You've got several other wives under thirty, Lula. What about Shirley or Mavis?"

Lula waved a hand dismissively, as if Wynn's suitability to the requirements was too obvious to waste breath on. Instead, she said, "Wynn, honey, you know if you don't want the job you have only to say so. That's one of the policies of Helpmates that I'm most proud of—one of the few real improvements over actual wifehood: the right to say no."

Wynn looked around the table uncertainly. "I think this man should call a casting agency and hire an actress."

Lula replied crisply, "Actually there's really nothing illegitimate about this request. I'd be the last to deny that a wife is a real asset in business. My husband would never have got where he did without my help, for instance."

Still uneasy about the assignment, Wynn seized on the hope that the time element was wrong. "When does he need someone?" she asked.

"Tonight," Lula replied. "And I think you should wear your hair pulled back like you sometimes do. That style makes your face look like a cameo. Very classy."

Turning to the person nearest to her own age of twenty-five, Wynn asked, "What do you think I should do, Jack?"

The blond young man unfolded his length from the oak chair and patted Wynn affectionately on the shoulder. "Take a chance, kid. You only live once. I know this sounds a lot flakier than our usual jobs, and I know our fair city is full of freaks and nuts, but it's also full of very interesting and creative people. If I were you, I'd jump at the chance of dinner at a classy French restaurant with a 'gentleman of means.' Give it a go, Wynn. But don't forget to take your police whistle along."

With that final bit of advice, Jack waved to them all and left to begin his work day. His departure reminded the others that they too must get going and in minutes Wynn and Lula were alone.

Wynn toyed with a few sweet-roll crumbs between her fingers. "The thing that bothers me about this job is the pretense. I can't remember that any of us has ever been asked to pretend to actually *be* someone's wife before, can you?"

"No," Lula replied promptly. "That's what put me off too, at first. But I checked him out with one of my sources. He's with an insurance company based in Sacramento. He's divorced and about a year ago, in the *Chronicle*'s society column, he was linked romantically with a woman executive here in San Francisco. As far as I can tell, he's legitimate."

"You want me to take the job, don't you?" Wynn asked, reassured now that she knew Lula had verified the man's

19

status. Also, she knew that Helpmates was not yet in a position to pick and choose too freely among job offers. It was no secret to any of the wives that Lula struggled valiantly and daily to keep the business out of the red. Each of them felt a loyalty to their plucky boss because, in spite of constant financial troubles, she paid each of them top dollar. It was another of Lula's policies that in wifery, above *all* occupations, the laborer was worthy of her hire. Or his, as the case might be.

"As I said earlier, honey, you're free to do what you think best, as always. I admit that yesterday, when I got word that we'd been turned down for that small-business loan, I might've been reluctant to turn down a job. Although," she added hastily, "I hope you know that even if I were on the brink of bankruptcy I'd never send one of my wives to an assignment I thought was dangerous."

"Of course I know that," Wynn assured the older woman. And Wynn did have perfect confidence in Lula's worldly experience and wisdom. Lula, after all, had been around.

Lula continued with a small, pleased smile on her bright lips. "But recently I met someone who I think will solve all our money problems for at least a year. In fact, today, for the first time in a year, I have very high hopes that we'll actually make a success of Helpmates!"

"Well, then . . ." Wynn said thoughtfully.

Taking Wynn's hesitation for acceptance, Lula briskly penciled in her name on the three-by-five card. "You know, honey, if you get any creepy vibes from him when he comes to pick you up, just refuse to go with him. Don't forget our motto: We can give you anything but love!"

As Wynn returned to the busy streets she made a mental inventory of her wardrobe. Was there anything suitable for the wife of a successful businessman to wear to an important business dinner at the glorious Le Bourgogne on a gala Saturday evening? Or should she, perhaps, treat herself to a new dress?

For a moment Wynn stood indecisively on the street corner, gently buffeted this way and that by the bustling throngs, wondering which way to go. Aware that she'd been pried loose from her inherently cautious and reserved nature, and glad of it, she smiled with expectation of the adventure awaiting her that evening and plunged into the flow of the city.

CHAPTER TWO

In a time when even two-income families were hard pressed to enter the housing market for the first time, Wynn Harris knew how fortunate she was to own outright a small, charming house in a quiet, humble residential section of one of the most expensive cities in the country. She had her hard-working mother to thank for it. Or, perhaps, to be fair, it was her scoundrel of a father to whom gratitude was owed. When he'd run off and abandoned his pregnant young wife so many years ago, he had at least left her with this house, mortgaged to the rafters though it had been at the time.

Now that Wynn was alone in the world and responsible for her own support, she thought often with awed respect of how desperately hard her mother must have worked to keep the two of them going, to maintain this roof over their heads, all those long, meager years of her childhood and early adolescence. And even more amazing, her mother had done it with such good cheer and grace that only since becoming an adult herself had Wynn realized that the world at large neither saw the dignity nor shared the respect for domestic work that her mother had felt and taught to Wynn.

What her mother had started out to do for the sake of love, she'd continued doing out of stark necessity. And now, in her mother's footsteps, but reversed, Wynn did the same work for pay that she yearned someday to do for love only.

Wynn wondered if her mother would recognize that Helpmates, Inc., was only a modern version of her own more monotonous daily work of cleaning other people's houses and washing other people's clothes. For instance, Wynn asked herself with an amused smile, what would her mother think of this evening's assignment?

She leaned closer to the pine-framed round mirror over the old-fashioned cabinet lavatory in her small outmoded bathroom and applied a light slick of Vaseline to her already thick enough dark eyelashes. After wiping her fingertips on a soft white hand towel, she smoothed back the glossy sweeps of dark hair that framed her lovely face and tucked an errant wisp into the coiled bun that rested above the tender young nape of her long, graceful neck.

All that remained was to slip on the dress she'd bought this afternoon with a guilty pleasure and a thankful thought for her charge card. The minute she'd seen it, Wynn had known the dress would lend her the confidence to play the part of a successful businessman's wife. At first glance it seemed a demure dress with its long, fitted chiffon sleeves and its high neckline nestled around her throat with a *faux* pearl-embroidered peter pan collar. But on second glance, and in spite of its pale pink color, there was nothing whatever girlish or innocent about the way the heavy silk bodice closely hugged the contours of Wynn's generously proportioned breasts or in the languid way the clouds of chiffon fell from the empire waist, skimming her rounded hips and playing about her shapely knees.

Actually it was quite a wicked dress, Wynn thought, smiling delightedly at the daring new self who looked back at her so confidently from the full-length mirror on the back of her bedroom closet door.

Wynn's husband for the evening obviously agreed, judging from his greeting when she opened her front door to

23

his knock a few minutes later. His eyes widened and he laughed nervously as he said, "Well, *Mrs. Packard*, you're even better than I'd hoped for."

The archness of his tone was slightly offputting, but first-time clients, male and female both, were often uncertain what attitude to take toward a hired wife, so the wives had all developed a certain tolerance and patience with such understandably anxious behavior.

Mr. Packard looked like any of the hundreds of businessmen Wynn saw every day in the city. He was nice enough looking, in his mid-fifties Wynn judged, of average height, and blessed with a full crop of healthy graying brown hair that he wore in a style that might have better become a man twenty years younger but was still within the bounds of propriety. However, the too youthful cut of his tan suit and brown-plaid vest did not become him at all. Wynn hoped that the blind spot that allowed him to wear the suit in the first place would also protect him from realizing it.

She gave him a friendly smile and a firm handshake, hoping to put him at his ease, then picked up her burgundy velveteen evening coat from the chair by the door. As she preceded Mr. Packard out the door of her house, Wynn fleetingly realized that her favorite musky perfume stood no chance this evening against the powerful aroma of his aftershave lotion.

As she stepped out into the soft summer air, Wynn was impressed to see a hired limousine with chauffeur double-parked at the curb. Grasping her elbow, Mr. Packard ushered her into the leather upholstered back seat, got in beside her, and closed the door with a satisfying click. As the long black car glided smoothly into the street, Wynn smiled, secretly feeling like a child on the way to the circus. She was just thinking that the evening was beginning like an adventure she would long remember with pleasure, when Mr. Packard suddenly turned toward her and firmly clamped a moist hand on her knee.

Wynn jerked to face him, her large, dark brown eyes staring in surprise, her soft mouth rounded open with alarm. Mr. Packard snatched back his hand as from an open flame and muttered, "Don't get in an uproar, honey. It looked like your skirt got hiked up and I was just pulling it down."

Wynn laughed shortly, then said in a clear, penetrating tone, "A feeble excuse is better than none, I suppose."

Mr. Packard leaned forward and forcefully closed the glass partition between the driver and the back seat, then leaned back and wedged himself tightly into the corner of the car. "I'm sorry, Miss ahh . . . Let's just forget it, okay?" he said sullenly.

Wynn took a deep breath so her voice wouldn't quaver and make her seem weak and afraid. "Mr. Packard, the office did make it clear to you that Helpmates is not a dating service or anything like that, didn't they?"

Cajolingly now, Mr. Packard replied, "I said I was sorry, didn't I, little lady?" Then, in a ponderously teasing tone, he added, "But I'll never understand why you girls go to so much trouble to look pretty if you don't want men to respond in a perfectly normal way."

As Wynn opened her mouth to reply, the man held up his hand like a traffic cop and said, "Never mind. I don't want to hear any of that women's lib propaganda. I'll behave if you'll just do your part when we get to the restaurant. You're supposed to be my adoring young wife. That's what I'm paying for, and that's what I expect to get."

More uneasy than she'd ever been during an assignment, Wynn considered asking the driver to pull over and let her out. She stole a glance at Mr. Packard and relaxed a bit to see that he was gazing blankly out the car window, ignoring her, seeming to be lost in his own thoughts.

Now that she was alerted to the type of man he was, what could actually happen? Certainly nothing further would happen in this car. Mr. Packard's closing of the partition glass showed that he was vulnerable to embarrassment, and that gave Wynn a powerful weapon. Surely he'd behave, for the same reason, in a public restaurant among his business associates. And if he drank so much during the evening that his embarrassment threshold was raised—and he seemed the sort to do just that—Wynn thought she could easily arrange to leave him outside the restaurant and go home alone in a cab.

Feeling better now that she'd worked out a contingency plan of escape, Wynn also felt less hostile toward Mr. Packard. Although she could never like him personally, she still felt obligated to give him good service for his money.

"Mr. Packard, would it help me to help you if I knew a bit more about why you hired me this evening?" Wynn asked in a businesslike way.

The man turned to look at her for a few seconds, as if considering his answer. Then a bitter smile flitted over his face and his tone was dry as he said, "Let's just say you're helping me tie up a few loose ends."

No wiser than before, Wynn said nothing more and for the rest of the trip to the restaurant there was no sound but the ordinary noises of any city, with the additional carnival clamor of San Francisco's cable car bells clanging in the distance, wisps and snatches of street music, and once, a throaty hoot from a passing freighter far away across the Bay.

Because none of the young men Wynn knew socially had yet reached the financial level necessary to patronize Le Bourgogne, she had never been inside, although she'd passed by its discreetly modest outer door on Elwood Lane off Mason Street many times. Now, on entering the dim hush of the famous restaurant, she was aware of an aura of sedate elegance. The many shimmering crystal chandeliers bathed the large quiet room in a glow flattering to the inhabitants, just as the soft sturdy carpet called no attention to itself so as not to compete with the guests' finery. Fresh flowers were in abundance everywhere. There were commodious tables in the center of the room, and hugging the walls was a series of intimate, cushiony banquettes upholstered in rose velvet.

It was to one of these that the headwaiter led Mr. Packard and Wynn. As they crossed the room Wynn noticed that more than a few of the other diners, especially the men, watched their progress with some interest. Wynn wondered why. Mr. Packard's too-youthful suit was not so inappropriate that he should excite such attention from Californians in general, not to mention San Franciscans in particular, who were accustomed to and tolerant of any and every style of dress.

But the thought was fleeting, for as they drew near their destination, Wynn's attention was diverted by the sudden rough touch of Mr. Packard's arm clutched familiarly around her slender waist. Into her ear he whispered a tense directive: "Remember now, you adore me."

Thoroughly rattled now, Wynn had no time to frame a reply before they reached the banquette and she was being introduced to two couples already seated. Smiling by reflex and shaking hands mechanically, Wynn scarcely took in anyone's face, much less did she remember anyone's name. When Mr. Packard finished the introductions to the first three people, he turned to the fourth, a tall, beautiful blonde in her mid-thirties. "Diane," he said in a low, tremulous voice, "how wonderful to see you again. You're looking ravishing."

The blonde's response was only mildly enthusiastic as she replied, "Nice to see you too, Buckie."

Mr. Packard then burdened Wynn's shoulders with his

heavy arm and with an odious smugness said, "Diane, this is my beautiful little bride."

The blonde's sharply plucked eyebrows arched over her cool blue eyes as she looked Wynn over, but her smile was kindly enough, in fact, Wynn thought, so kind it might have been construed as pitying. "She certainly *is* a beauty, Buckie. Enchanted to meet you, my dear. I'm sorry, I didn't hear your name."

Mr. Packard—Buckie, rather—threw his little bride a panicked look; and in that split second Wynn remembered that she was not at all powerless against this sad and ridiculous bully who'd hired her services for the evening. Knowing this, her healthy self-regard and inherent self-confidence came flooding back. She said with a friendly, composed smile, "My name is Wynn," and remembered just in time not to add Harris.

When the preliminaries were finally over, Wynn took notice of the others at the table. Near the middle of the banquette's U shape sat a congenial-looking couple. The woman had a sweetly rounded face topped by a cluster of light brown curls, giving the impression of a toothsome cupcake frosted with burnt-sugar icing. The man, whom Wynn took to be the young woman's husband, had merry blue eyes and sported a neatly trimmed ginger-colored beard and moustache. On Wynn's right, at one end of the banquette, was Mr. Buckie Packard, now gazing with mournful eyes at the self-contained Diane across from him.

Wynn was wedged in so tightly between Mr. Packard and the man on her left that she couldn't see him well, so her impression of him was sketchy. When he'd stood for the introductions, she'd seen he was tall and rangy. From the well-manicured, sinewy fingers of the hand that lay composedly beside her on the white linen tablecloth, Wynn judged him to be fastidious. The subtle almond scent that emanated from him and the impeccable tailor-

ing of his dove-gray suit suggested that he was discriminating and austere in his tastes. Altogether he gave
off an aura of such self-assurance as to verge on arrogance.
Probably he was a San Franciscan of that certain type
whose comings and goings were breathlessly related to the
masses in the newspapers' society columns.

"You haven't been married long, I take it." The man's
voice startled Wynn, coming from so deep in his chest as
it did, and yet in such a velvety, intimate tone as if not
meant as a contribution to the general conversation but for
her ears alone. Wynn turned to look at him and nearly
gasped aloud at the impact his eyes made on her. Never
before had she seen eyes of such a remarkable color—a
deep, glowing sable brown with a tinge of purple around
the iris. "What?" Wynn breathed inelegantly.

"Because our Buckie seemed not to know your name,"
the man added with a strange smile on his wide, full lips.

Wynn's heart thudded uncomfortably. She clenched her
hands in her lap, whether to repress a sudden wild desire
to run her finger down the graceful slope of his high-
bridged aquiline nose, or because of the exposure the
man's statement seemed to threaten, she couldn't tell.

Because her throat felt tight, Wynn's voice was breathy
as she replied with a savoir faire she didn't feel, "Of course
Mr.—*Buckie* knows my name. He was simply letting me
speak for myself, as a husband should."

The man's smile was sardonic now. "Bride, or not, now
I *know* you haven't known 'Mr. Buckie' very long. He's
not the type to let any woman speak for herself unless he's
certain she means to say yes."

Wynn was spared thinking of a reply to this suggestive
remark when Mr. Packard, hearing his name, turned to
the dark man at Wynn's side and said jovially, "Well,
Aaron, what do you think of my little pigeon? Isn't she a
knockout?"

Aaron looked at Wynn with an appraising gaze from his

29

sensually lidded, compelling eyes. "Indeed she is, Buckie. One can always count on you to come up with just the right package for any situation, but this time I do believe you've surpassed yourself."

With a hearty laugh Mr. Packard replied, "Let's hope you remember that when those policies of yours come up for renewal next month!"

Wynn's blush of anger at being discussed like an item of merchandise no doubt went unseen in the low romantic light of the chandeliers overhead, and she was grateful when the conversation turned from her to more general talk. As she listened to the others, she pieced together that Anne, the pretty brown-haired woman, was the dark man's sister and that the ginger-bearded man was indeed her husband. The three of them, and the cool blonde, too, seemed to be involved in some business together. Judging from Mr. Packard's deferential, not to say sycophantic, manner toward them all, Wynn guessed that they were all highly prized customers of his, and that Buckie was the evening's host. What her own part in all this was intended to be was still as great a mystery to Wynn as ever.

When the waiter came to take the orders for dinner, he seemed to assume that Aaron was host. And after a brief consultation, the other diners as well decided to leave it all to the dark man, and Wynn was not surprised to see how naturally he took charge.

"We'll have the Little Neck clams on the half shell for the first course. For the entree, four medaillons of beef." Then, indicating Wynn with an elegant hand, he added, "This lady and I will share the beef Wellington for two. Hearts of palm salad to follow, and we'll order dessert later. Tell the wine steward to bring us two bottles of the Beaulieu Private Reserve Cabernet Sauvignon, '41 if you have them; if not, the '51 will do."

Wynn felt Mr. Packard, close at her side, start as if from a blow. Even Wynn knew enough to guess what aged

30

vintage wine might cost, and in spite of her dislike of Mr. Packard, she felt sympathy for him as the pirate on her left figuratively rifled Buckie's wallet.

For her own part Wynn felt both taken aback and uneasy at the news that she would share a dinner with the dark man, and she noticed that the blonde, Diane, as well, seemed to take it poorly. Projecting across the table a look that, on a less sophisticated face, might have been a glare, Diane said in a frosty and enigmatically meaningful tone, "You certainly know how to order what you want, don't you, Aaron?"

With a brief, bland smile, Aaron replied unperturbably, "I feel in the mood for beef Wellington this evening and it's more convenient to share a dish for two with the person sitting next to me. I felt sure our Mrs. Packard would have no objection. Do you, little bride?" he asked Wynn suddenly, throwing her off-balance as she felt again the full impact of those glowing eyes.

"Of course she doesn't mind," Buckie answered for her quickly. "She's the sweetest, most pliable little wife a man could ever want." He glanced covertly at Diane. "Aren't you . . . sweetie?" he asked Wynn and she knew that he'd forgotten her name again.

Leaning across Wynn to speak directly to Buckie, Aaron said in a bland tone, "Sweetie's name is Wynn, Buckie. It's so easy to forget these outlandish names girls give themselves nowadays."

Wynn felt her face grow hot at this throwing down of the gauntlet. There was no mistaking the hostility and contempt in the awful man's words. He knew she was not Buckie's wife—she shuddered even to contemplate what he *did* think she was—and he wanted to make sure *Wynn* knew that he knew. She sat frozen in miserable embarrassment, paralyzed by her ignorance of the meaning of this impossible situation she found herself in.

Aaron's sister, Anne, threw her brother a disapproving

31

look, then sweetly gave Wynn her full attention. "Max and I have friends in Fair Oaks, Wynn. Do you and Buckie live anywhere near that part of Sacramento?"

Wynn's heart plunged in dismay. She knew nothing whatever about Sacramento save that it was the state capital. But Buckie saved the day by replying for her. "We live in that fabulous new condo development on the bluffs overlooking the American River, Anne." Then, turning again to Diane, he asked lugubriously, "You remember the day you and I looked those over, don't you, Diane, honey?"

"I'm hardly likely to forget that day, Buckie." Then as if taking pity on him, she added lukewarmly, "They're very nice condominiums . . . for Sacramento."

By the time the waiter took away the empty plates from the first course, Wynn had grown aware of two factors guaranteed to destroy her appetite and cinch her already taut nerves one more notch: first, Buckie Packard, she now realized, had not been sober when he'd picked her up earlier this evening—hence the overdose of shaving lotion —and he was even less so now, and growing more erratic and emotional by the wineglass, second, Wynn finally understood that she'd been brought along this evening for the pitiful and futile purpose of making the cool, lofty Diane jealous—to punish her for the grievous wound she'd inflicted on Buckie when she'd removed herself from his life.

When the entrees were brought to the table, Wynn was served a succulent slice of pink beef wrapped in a flaky pastry crust. At any other time she would have made short work of it. But now she merely pushed the accompanying browned new potatoes around on her plate and listened as the others discussed an ever-popular subject in San Francisco: the cost of real estate.

As if the two of them were alone at the table, Aaron leaned close and whispered in Wynn's ear, "Eat your dinner, pretty one. Your 'husband' is paying good money for it—and lots of it."

Wynn heard the sarcasm in his voice and she looked up to see the knowing smile flickering in his dark eyes. "Here, taste this," he coaxed. "Just a little bite."

Taken by surprise and confused by Aaron's closeness, Wynn automatically obeyed by opening her mouth and receiving the tidbit of meat proffered on the tines of Aaron's fork. When the soft-as-butter meat nestled onto her taste buds, Wynn felt the most delicious flood of warmth and pleasure travel from her throat down into her stomach. She looked up guiltily—although she couldn't have said why—to see Aaron's sister watching them with a thoughtful look in her eyes.

From the right Wynn heard an ugly explosive snort from Buckie. "You like the pretty little bird, don't you, Aaron? You're planning to steal her away from me, aren't you? Just the way you stole Diane."

A shocked silence settled over the table until Diane found her voice and said with angry weariness, "Oh, *spare* me, Buckie. You know it wasn't anything like that. Can't you face reality just once in your life?"

Buckie's face was red and distorted now as he leaned across Wynn as if she weren't there and said in a voice thick with rage, "Behold the man who has everything! Wealth, background, education, good looks—and yet, with all that, he's not man enough to find his own women. He has to steal other men's women—"

"Shut your stupid, drunken mouth, Buckie," Aaron cut in, his voice hard enough to pulverize diamonds. "No one could have stolen Diane from you, since you never had her. And as for her"—he gestured toward a trembling Wynn—"she reminds me of the old joke: Who was that lady I saw you with last night? Remember? Only in this case it's Who was that wife I saw you with last night? That was no wife, that was a lady! A *hired* lady," Aaron

33

sneered, "unless I've misjudged you and you've finally found a woman dumb enough to get involved in one of your rotten schemes for free!"

Buckie emitted a snarl of outrage and threw a wild punch past a horrified Wynn. In seconds a covey of black-garbed waiters descended on the table and Buckie was removed from his seat and surrounded like a sardine. With impassive faces and ruthless Gallic efficiency, the waiters ushered a blubbering Buckie from the dining room to some private place in the back reaches of the restaurant.

CHAPTER THREE

Wynn scrambled toward the now empty end of the banquette, pushing against the table to escape, hearing but not heeding the tinkling crash of a knocked-over wineglass. Stiff with shock and inflamed with mortification, she cared for nothing but to leave this place and these people—never to set foot in here again or lay eyes on these faces.

"Wynn, wait . . . wait!" She identified Anne's concerned voice calling out amid the excited babble of the other diners as she ran blindly through the great room and out the door into the damp, chill August night. She plunged into a taxi miraculously cruising by, slammed the door, and pushed down the lock button. As the cab pulled away from the curb she glanced back fearfully, and there was that devil, that monster, bursting from the restaurant's doorway, waving her evening coat at the end of one long arm and shouting words she couldn't hear. Shuddering, she cringed back against the cracked, smoke-soaked leather seat and buried her face in her hands.

Wynn felt such a welter of nasty emotions and her mind was so distracted by bitter thoughts, she was quite unable to decide which man to hate the most: Mr. Packard for making use of her, without her knowledge, for his stupid, low purpose of revenge, or that Aaron's cynical assumption that if she wasn't exactly what she was purported to be, she must therefore be a prostitute.

The cabbie's laconic tone cut through her hot, angry thoughts. "Some guy give you a hard time, doll?"

Seizing on his comment, Wynn thought furiously, *There it is again! That disgusting male attitude that women are the common property of men, mere playthings; not individual people at all! Honey. Sweetie. Little lady, little bride, little pigeon.* Even a hired driver, on two seconds acquaintance, felt free to call her "doll." Only when she'd suddenly become a possession, a belonging to lay claim to, had either man in the restaurant lent her the dignity of being named a *woman.* And even that had been insulting, Wynn thought bitterly. She'd known neither of them for more than an hour—and yet both of them had taken it for granted that she could be used as a pawn in what was obviously an ongoing rivalry between them for Diane's affections.

In the dark solitude of the stuffy cab, Wynn grimaced in self-disgust to remember that secret thrill of excitement, that powerful surge of interest that she'd felt at the moment when she'd first looked into that horrible man's seductive eyes. How treacherous they all were! But, no. Wynn pressed her lips into a tight, determined line with the effort to be fair. Not *all* men were rotters. Just most of them—like those two marauders in the restaurant and even . . . her own father.

But there were also good men. Men who were real people. Men like sweet Ed Patterson, and Professor Jenkins, and Jack Clancey, who, although still very young, showed no signs at all of turning into a miserable wretch like that Aaron.

Wynn was just wondering why Aaron's disgusting assumptions and insulting remarks were beginning to seem more unforgivable than Buckie Packard's hiring her for such a demeaning purpose, when the cabbie spoke to her over his shoulder. "I think you're being followed, sweetheart."

Wynn's heart leaped in alarm as she twisted around to peer out the back window. It was dark now, and she could see little but the blazing headlights of a vehicle close on the cab's tail. Looking out the side window, she saw that she was in her own neighborhood, within a few blocks of her house. Searching the seat beside her for her handbag, she said to the driver in a breathless voice, "If you'll just walk me to my door, I think everything will be all right."

The driver hesitated, then shrugged. "If it's just a . . . like, lovers' quarrel, I guess I don't mind. But otherwise, I mean if it's anything heavy, I don't want to get involved. I'll drive you to the nearest police station, doll, but that's it. Okay?"

Wynn glared at his back. Fuming with impotent rage, despising her need of his protection, she choked out, "Yes, it's just a lovers' quarrel."

As the driver deftly swung the cab to the curb and braked to a rocking halt, Wynn realized with a sinking heart that her handbag was nowhere on the seat. In fact, it was not in the cab at all, but either back at Le Bourgogne, or worse yet, like the velveteen coat she thought she'd never see again, in the clutches of the man who was at that very moment leaping from the cab behind her and closing in on her fast.

The driver got out of the cab as Aaron strode over and said to him, "I'll take over from here, Mac." He handed the cabbie a folded bill of unknown denomination, then opened the back door and reached a long arm in to grasp Wynn by the elbow. In a tone that bespoke both intimacy and long-suffering patience, he said, "Come on now, darling. Let's go inside and finish our discussion in private."

To give the driver what little credit he deserved, he did peer into the back seat with an eyebrow raised in question to Wynn, sitting stiffly on the edge of the seat. When she only stared back at him blankly—what on earth could she say?—he seemed satisfied. With a shrug he withdrew his head.

Feeling her resistance, Aaron then poked his head into the cab's murky interior and hissed through clenched teeth, "Get out here instantly, or you're going to be sorry." Then in a switch that would have made Jekyll and Hyde green with envy, he looked over his shoulder at the driver and with a man-to-man smile, said, "You just never know what little thing will set them off into a tizzy, do you?"

The driver laughed, leaned against the cab, and lit a cigarette. "You know it, man. Chicks are really something else, ain't they?"

With a deep sigh of resignation, Wynn got out of the cab and watched stoically as the knight in yellow armor drove off, leaving her to the uncertain mercies of Aaron, who now pushed her own handbag at her and ordered her to get out the key to her own front door.

Turning her back on him to do so, Wynn said flatly, "Too bad you let both cabs leave. They don't cruise in this neighborhood, so you'll have to walk now."

As she turned the key in the lock and pushed open her front door, Aaron said with such smooth assurance that they might've been the best of friends, "I'll just come in for a moment and call for one."

Wynn stepped up into her entry hall and turned to face him, now level with his hateful, smirking, handsome face. With frigid implacability she said, "Not on my phone, you won't."

Aaron smiled unpleasantly. "Don't worry, I'll pay for the call. I realize you require payment for all your . . . favors," he said, his tone giving the word a sordid connotation.

At this shockingly hostile remark sudden tears stung Wynn's eyes and her heart filled with a terrible ache. To hide her pain, to retaliate in kind, Wynn lifted her chin

38

haughtily. "*You* don't have enough money to pay for my favors."

Aaron raised one dark, thick eyebrow and smiled sardonically. "Ah, then I'm right. It isn't a question of payment, per se; it's just a question of how much. Is that right?"

His further insult changed Wynn's hurt to fury—fury at herself as well as him. Why should she care what he thought? Why should she allow the sick, nasty assumptions of this arrogant stranger to cause her such pain?

"That's correct," Wynn replied coldly. "But for *you*, no amount would be enough. Now please give me my coat and go away."

Aaron pulled his arm back just enough to place Wynn's coat out of her reach. "Now you're contradicting yourself, little bride. For someone of your . . . calling, anything's for sale—to anyone—if the price is right."

Fed up to the teeth with his cruelly teasing game, Wynn made a grab for her coat and in that second when she was off-balance, Aaron seized hold of her around the waist, stepped up into her entry hall, and closed the front door behind him. Frightened now, and fully aware of how much bigger and stronger than she he was, Wynn tried to twist away from him. "Get out of here and leave me alone!" she cried in a tight, choked voice.

As if she'd never spoken, Aaron held her tightly and drawled, "Or maybe you're telling me that your favors are priceless." He looked down at Wynn with a luminous glow in his dark, heavily fringed eyes. "That I'd believe." Then like a dark cloud his lean face descended, and his firm, wide mouth covered Wynn's lips.

Her eyes flew wide open in alarm and she pushed against his hard chest to escape, but in one swift movement he threw her coat toward a nearby chair, pulled both her arms down to her sides, and pinned them there with his strong, muscular arms. His kiss was hard, angry, pun-

39

ishing. Wynn twisted her head violently from side to side to escape it. When he briefly raised his mouth from hers, Wynn gasped out weakly, "Let me go! How dare you . . ."

Aaron suddenly released her arms and Wynn felt a second's surprised relief that he'd heeded her demand. But her freedom was short-lived, for he'd loosened his grip on her only to achieve a better purchase. With a quick movement he encircled her hips and pulled her against him while with his other hand he cupped the base of her head in an immobilizing grasp. Again he lowered his mouth to hers, and the firmness of his kiss deepened and yet softened as he lightly stroked the sensitive membrane of Wynn's inner lips with the warm, moist tip of his tongue.

Captured there in Aaron's arms, helpless to escape, Wynn felt his heat through the gauzy chiffon of her dress. As she became aware of what she muzzily identified as the elevator feeling, that oddly pleasant sensation in her stomach of falling from a great height, her agitated body stopped its struggle and grew still.

When Aaron felt Wynn's form slacken and melt into his, he loosened his hold on her head, trailed his fingertips languidly down the soft skin of her neck, then spread his palm like a warm blanket over the silk bodice of her dress, coming to rest at her side, tantalizingly close to the firm fullness of her breast. With a small, involuntary moan she arched herself against him. As Aaron's lips left her mouth to nuzzle at the sensitive place where her ear lobe met her cheek, Wynn shivered. His movement released a fresh, pungent scent of almond to assail her nostrils, and his breath was hot on her ear as he whispered huskily, "You're right to hold yourself so dear, little bride, if this is a fair sample of your wares."

As this further insult brought reality crashing back, Wynn stiffened with horror to realize that her body had betrayed her by reacting with such pleasure and desire to a man so thoroughly unpleasant and undesirable as this one. With a resolve born of wounded self-esteem, she gave him a hard push and scuttled to the center of her living room a few steps away.

She snatched up her coat from the floor where he'd tossed it and held it clasped in front of her like a shield, as if to protect her trembling body from the assault of his dark, knowing gaze. Aaron stood insouciantly where she'd left him in the foyer. With one well-defined eyebrow arched in sardonic query, he remarked, "Isn't a display of righteous indignation a little inappropriate, under the circumstances?"

Wynn's lips parted to tell him how mistaken he was, to put an end to this farce, but before she could speak, he continued in a smug, chiding tone. "Especially after what I've done for you this evening."

A sound of choked astonishment escaped from Wynn's throat. "What you've done for me! What you've done *to* me is insult me, pursue me, break into my house, and attack me!"

"Is that how you see it?" he asked with seemingly honest surprise. "Then that just verifies my earlier conviction that you're a rotten judge of character."

Nonplused at this man's truly monumental arrogance, Wynn's frustration overwhelmed her good sense and she retorted tauntingly, "I'm not such a rotten judge of character that I wouldn't rather be embarrassed by Buckie Packard than be kissed by you!"

Aaron's response was a short, incredulous laugh. "Who do you think you're kidding? I was *there,* if you recall. I saw your response to him—and you were mortified, not embarrassed." Then, jabbing down at the foyer floor with his long, slender index finger at a point a bare inch from where he stood, he drawled suggestively, "And I was *here.* I didn't notice you knocking over any tables in your haste to run out *this* front door."

"This is *my house*," she cried out in a voice nearly strangled with outrage.

"And even if you did mean what you said, and you know you don't, it would only prove me right again," he added smugly.

Enraged that he'd had the gall to mention her inexplicable physical response to him right out in public like that, so to speak, and stinging from humiliation that he'd so easily laughed away what she'd thought was a killingly odious comparison between him and Buckie, Wynn was wild to wipe that righteous smirk from Aaron's face.

Grabbing the only weapon at hand, Wynn reared back and with a mighty heave flung her coat across the room at him, shouting, "Just get out of here before I call the police!" Then she watched with hopeless dismay as the heavy velveteen cloth slithered harmlessly in a heap at his feet. With a fluid, graceful motion Aaron absentmindedly scooped up the coat and tossed it onto one of the sofas flanking Wynn's fireplace. Shaking his dark head mournfully, Aaron intoned, "And this is the thanks I get for rescuing you from a fate worse than death."

Putting on a hard, jeering attitude, Wynn retorted, "Too bad your *gallantry* has all been for naught, Mr. Galahad, but I don't need you or anyone else to rescue me. I can take care of myself very well."

Then she was taken aback to see the change that came over Aaron's face at her flip, offhand jibe. Unknowingly, it seemed she'd at last struck a nerve. Gone was the slightly playful smile, gone the amused light in his dark, sable eyes. And in spite of all the insults and nasty innuendos he'd arrowed her way all evening, she now saw for the first time a look of real disapproval and censure on his stern face.

"That's what they all say nowadays," he said snidely, "until the going gets rough. Look, little bride, I can tell you're new at this. And I really don't think you're suited

42

to it either. "Take my advice"—he smiled in a sinister way—"give it up before you get hurt. Get into some honest line of work until Mr. Right comes along and marries you. That's obviously what you're cut out for."

Again Wynn heard the querulous little voice within her ask why this man should arouse such violent emotions? Why should his assessment of her, wrong though it was, cause her such distress?

An image of sweet, kind Ed Patterson suddenly shimmered in her mind, and Wynn said defiantly, "I've already found my Mr. Right. And you'd better get out of here immediately . . ." she warned ominously. Then ostentatiously raising her wrist to eye level, she glanced at it imperiously, only to discover too late that she wasn't wearing her wrist watch. Since there was nothing else to do, she plunged on. ". . . or in five minutes he'll be here to throw you out," she finished lamely.

After a moment's hesitation in which Wynn saw a look of startled uncertainty flash across Aaron's face, he responded with a contemptuous snort. "So much for your taking care of yourself," he scoffed. "You women are all alike. You demand equality and independence and then as soon as something doesn't go your way, you start screeching for some man to save you."

Wynn's mouth dropped open in astonishment. What hysterical, illogical creatures men were! Obviously she'd never get rid of this maniac until she gave him what he wanted. Her shoulders slumped in defeat. She sighed heavily in resignation. "All right, I've had all I'm going to take of this foolishness. Make your phone call and then get out of here."

Ignoring her offer, Aaron went on sarcastically. "And if there *is* a Mr. Right—which I doubt—he can't be very right in the head to allow you to do this kind of work."

Wynn felt a flush of color creep into her cheeks as she realized he'd seen through her transparent fib. But at her reaction Aaron's eyes narrowed in suspicion. "Or maybe he doesn't know what you do. That's it, isn't it?" he demanded harshly. "You just *use* him. You take what you can get from him, just like all the others."

At this latest effrontery the entire scenario of this sordid evening from beginning to the present swirled through Wynn's mind as if on a runaway film clip, and her normally large brown eyes slitted with fury. She advanced on Aaron with clenched fists, enraged beyond good sense and fearless now. "You miserable wretch," she cried, marching around him and throwing open her front door with a flourish. "Get out of my sight!"

Aaron shrugged insolently and in an infuriatingly slow, lazy stroll approached the door. "And never darken your door again?" He smiled mockingly.

"Just get out," Wynn repeated, flattening herself against the entry wall so as not to come in contact with his large, muscular body—ever again!

As Aaron briefly lounged against the door frame, he gave her a thin, grim smile. "Well, I won't say it hasn't been an interesting evening," he drawled, "but don't call me—I'll call you. That *is* how you run your business, isn't it?" With that parting shot he gave Wynn a mock salute and turned to lope away into the night. By the time she recovered her wits enough to slam the door in his hateful face, he was half a block away.

CHAPTER FOUR

Never before had Ed Patterson looked as good to Wynn as he did the following day as she sat at the tiny kitchen table in his studio apartment overlooking the city's marina. In contrast to that uncivilized maniac last night, Ed looked comfortingly domestic in his white cotton baker's apron with the motto I'D RATHER BE PLAYING TENNIS emblazoned in red block letters on the front. There was something very appealing in the frown of concentration on Ed's brow as he organized the various oven times and temperatures required to cook the frozen gourmet foods that were the full extent of his culinary repertoire.

Ed turned to give Wynn a slow, wistful smile as he said, "I like it when you come for Sunday brunch, Wynn. It reminds me of the good times in my married life."

As Wynn returned his smile, some part of her mind, against her will, insisted on comparing Ed's boyish face and clear blue eyes with Aaron's elegant, sardonic face and dark, compelling eyes. Shivering slightly to shake the unwelcome image, Wynn replied gently, "You really miss marriage, don't you, Ed."

"Well, yes. But that's not the reason I want you to marry me. And it isn't the kids either." Ed took the few steps between the kitchen counter and the table where Wynn sat and leaned over to kiss her on the brow. "I want you for yourself, Wynn," he said softly.

Wynn's heart ached with sympathy for him. She longed

to be able to return his feelings, and it worried and baffled her that she just couldn't. Wasn't he exactly what she wanted in a man? Wasn't he kind and gentle? Amusing? Didn't he have a faithful nature and a natural feeling for children? And, as for the less important but very pleasant qualities to be found in a man, he was good-looking and seemed to have a successful career ahead of him. In just a few years he would be a full partner in his law firm. Nor did he have any vices—unless a passion for tennis could be called a vice!

And yet her feelings for Ed during the year she'd known him had never developed beyond a warm affection—an emotion she imagined one might feel toward a cousin or a brother-in-law—neither of which Wynn had. And to make it all even more baffling, today she couldn't seem to stop comparing him unfavorably to that rude, snide wretch she'd had the misfortune to clash with last night and—thank heaven!—would never see again as long as she lived.

To compensate for the lack of feeling she so regretted, Wynn doubled her efforts to be a congenial companion to Ed that afternoon. She heaped generous praise on the frozen chicken crepes, spinach soufflé, fruit cup, and brown-and-serve rolls Ed served for brunch. She listened with close attention to the lengthy recital of last week's tennis tournament at the tennis club he belonged to. When he suggested a walk to the coffee house that he frequented on the wharf, she acquiesced even though she didn't much care for that area of the city, where crowds of tourists thronged the streets.

Even so, Wynn had to admit that the view of the passing parade from the patio of the coffee house was charming in its color and variety. The low afternoon sun bathed the world in an intensely golden light and the fresh, pungent breeze from the sea was exhilarating. Wynn and Ed sat at a rococo wrought iron table sipping from cups of creamy cappuccino while people of all ages and descriptions streamed past. Tourists, many laden with purchases from the exotic shops abounding, gawked, pointed, laughed, and smiled with delight as they ate out-of-hand fresh seafood bought from the many stalls lining the street. San Franciscans, in their motley modes of dress, from impeccable heathery tweeds to jeans and T-shirts to sleazy gauze harem pants, strolled by like benign royalty in the city's uniquely insouciant manner.

"It's like a medieval bazaar, isn't it?" Wynn mused.

From several blocks away the clang of a cable car's bell announced its arrival at the foot of the hill as Ed replied wistfully, "I wish the kids were here today."

Wynn patted his hand reassuringly. "They'll be here next weekend, won't they?"

"That's right. You have us down on your work schedule, don't you?"

Wynn laughed. "Absolutely. You don't think I'd overlook my favorite assignment, do you?"

Ed said eagerly, "Say, why don't we take them to the wax museum next week. They're old enough now, don't you think?"

Wynn considered, frowning slightly, thinking of eight-year-old Peter, shy and a bit timid for his age, and little Tara, only six. "Only if we can steer them away from the bloodier exhibits, Ed. Even *I'm* not old enough for Jack the Ripper!"

"Well, we'll see," Ed said vaguely, reaching over to enfold Wynn's hands in his own. The look in his guileless blue eyes was that of unabashed longing as he murmured, "Oh, Wynn, if only you'd say yes—right now—I know I could make you happy, and the kids love you as much as I do. And you love them. I know you do from the way you are with them."

As though to painlessly stifle Ed's words, Wynn leaned quickly across the small table and lightly covered Ed's lips with her own. She was aware that she felt only the hard metal edge of the table pressing into her diaphragm and its coolness through the thin gingham of her red-and-white checked shirt. These were not the sort of feelings she'd had last night when another man had kissed her.

"Please, Ed," she murmured, "of course I love the children. And you know how fond I am of you . . ." Wynn reached up to smooth back the sandy cowlick that eternally fell over Ed's forehead. "But I guess I'm just not ready yet. I'm sorry."

From somewhere above and behind the table where they sat, a hearty voice caroled out, "Wynn! Ed! Fancy meeting you here!" And descending on them like a gaily decked out tugboat came Lula Dobbs accompanied by a slim, pretty redhaired girl and—to Wynn's total shock and consternation—looming like a tall-masted schooner behind the two women, the dark stranger whose assaultive kiss she'd thought of with such guilty pleasure just seconds before.

All the color and variety and noise of the street disappeared for Wynn, and she was aware, as in a dream, only of the man's aristocratic face, his smoldering eyes, his wide mouth quirked at the corners in a dry smile, his dark, wavy hair glinting with fiery lights in the molten rays of the setting sun.

Tearing her gaze from his with an effort, Wynn turned her scrambled attention to Lula, who was chattering on in her usual blithe manner. "How wonderful to see you! May we join you?" Without waiting for the answer she took for granted, she gestured for the pretty redhaired girl and the dark man to make their way through the crowded patio to take a seat at the next table, a foot away from where Wynn and Ed sat.

Aaron, in a drawled demur, said, "I think we're interrupting a tête-à-tête, Ms. Dobbs. I feel sure these people would rather . . . carry on . . . alone."

48

Wynn flushed at his *double entendre,* knowing it meant he'd seen her kiss Ed and put his own sick interpretation on it. Lula laughed boisterously and flapped a small, soft hand in dismissal. "No, no, no, they won't mind. Sit down, sit down!"

With a nearly imperceptible shrug, Aaron moved his long, rangy body sideways behind Wynn's chair to reach the small empty table near Wynn that Lula indicated. As his flat belly and hard thighs brushed against Wynn's shoulders she felt the flesh of her upper arms, thankfully covered by her long sleeves, erupt in shivery goosebumps.

While one of Lula's arms windmilled for the waiter, with the other she waved out introductions. "Wynn, Ed, this is Meg, my darling granddaughter."

As the pretty young girl smiled shyly, Lula added in a meaningful aside to Wynn, "You've heard me speak of Meg often lately, Wynn dear." Then she went on. "This gentleman is Mr. A. J. Stone. Mr. Stone, Ed Patterson was one of Helpmates' first clients. I'm sure he'll give us good references, won't you, Ed? And Wynn Harris is one of my most valuable employees."

At Lula's remark, a marble mask suddenly hardened over Aaron Stone's face and he stared first at Lula and then at Wynn with a shuttered look in his dark eyes. Ed offered a hand to Aaron, who, after a second's hesitation, shook it perfunctorily. With a curt nod to Wynn, he asked Lula blandly, "This young woman works for you, you say?"

Lula nodded, beaming proudly.

"In what capacity?" Aaron asked bluntly.

While Wynn blanched, Lula answered blithely, "Why, as one of my wives! One of the very best, too, I might add."

Aaron sank back against the metal back of the chair as if to remove himself from the circle of people and Ed sat up stiffly, as if to make himself taller. Blissfully unaware, Lula trilled on as the waiter brought fresh cups of steaming coffee and a plate of pastries. "There now, isn't this lovely that we should all happen to run into each other on such a superb day? Mr. Stone and I had a long-standing business appointment today, but when Meg so unexpectedly—and delightfully!—drove in from Palo Alto, we all decided to mix business with pleasure."

"Just as you and Mr. Patterson are doing, isn't that right, Ms. Harris?" Aaron interjected silkily.

With a surly brusqueness completely unlike him, Ed spoke up. "It's true that Ms. Harris and I do have a standing business arrangement once a month, Mr. Stone, but it just so happens that today is purely a social occasion."

Aaron Stone said insinuatingly, "You see, Ms. Dobbs, I was right: we have interrupted a tête-à-tête, as I said. And I'm right again, Mr. Patterson, that you and Ms. Harris are mixing business with pleasure—for what could be more obvious than that any business dealings with a woman as lovely as she must be a pleasure?" Turning to Lula, he said almost accusingly, "So much for that we-can-give-you-anything-but-love hogwash of yours, Ms. Dobbs."

Now Lula's soft, full face hardened too, for Aaron Stone had deeply offended her by questioning the integrity of her business and, thus, her own. "I assure you, Mr. Stone, you've misunderstood the situation. If Ms. Harris and Mr. Patterson have a friendship I've not been aware of, I'm sure that's their own affair—er, business. But as for their business arrangement"—Lula stopped briefly, looking puzzled by her own explanation—"that's strictly business."

Now Ed spoke up again, his sandy hair fairly bristling with indignation, looking like a fledgling bird confronting a hawk. "I think you owe Ms. Harris an apology, Mr. Stone."

With a brief glance in Ed's direction, Aaron said coolly,

"If I should ever come to share your opinion, Mr. Patterson, I'll be only too willing to apologize to Ms. Harris." Then his dark gaze swung to fix directly on a pale Wynn as he added, "But in the meantime, only the greatest of fools would deny the possibility of fire when so much smoke is in evidence." Then turning to Lula, he said, "Ms. Dobbs, if you'll excuse me, I have another appointment. Since it's within walking distance, please allow my driver to see you and Meg home."

Lula's soft, silly loveableness had gone into hiding, leaving at the fore all the dignity and hard-earned self-respect that had kept her on life's crest for so many years. "That won't be necessary, Mr. Stone. I've gotten around this city without your driver for a long time now, and I'll get around it without him in the future too."

With hooded eyes Aaron Stone gave a short nod to Lula and the others and turned on his heel to walk away.

Meg broke the silence. "You were super, Ed," she breathed admiringly. "I think it was wonderful the way you defended Wynn's honor like that."

Ed turned to look at her fresh, young face. With a puzzled frown he said, "Actually, I'm not really sure he attacked Wynn's honor—it's just that it sounded so insulting the way he said it."

Wynn, staring stolidly down into her cooling coffee, did not suffer Ed's doubt that Aaron Stone had indeed intended to attack her honor. However, she wanted no apology from him, nor anything else, unless she might be granted the wish that he disappear into thin air and never be heard from again. That would go far toward making the world a happier place!

"Well, whatever he was talking about, *I* think you were *heroic*, Ed, I really do," Meg said warmly.

Gradually the frown of puzzlement left Ed's face and he grinned broadly. "Really? Well"—he shrugged modestly —"it was the least I could do, after all."

Lula leaned her elbows on the table and blew absently into the cup she held in both hands. "I just can't understand what set him off," she said musingly. "I haven't known him long, it's true, but I'd never have thought he'd behave so oddly."

Wynn emitted a long, gusty sigh. "At least you found out what he's really like before he was inflicted on one of the wives," she said with great feeling, remembering her own fresh affliction from one Buckie Packard.

"He was awfully handsome, though, wasn't he?" Meg commented timidly.

"And so rich," Lula added mournfully.

Wynn gasped indignantly. "What's wrong with you two anyway! Handsome is as handsome does! And since when does it matter if a client is rich! In fact, as our resident Marxist, Paul so often points out that generally speaking the richer they are, the more arrogant, unfair, and demanding they are. And that beast just proves it!" Wynn suddenly stopped, aware that her voice had risen to such a shrill pitch that passersby were stopping to stare.

"We came down to the wharf today," Lula began in a thoughtful, faraway tone, "because I thought it would amuse Meg while we talked business—and he wanted to show me how he's handled some of his other ventures. He owns three shops in the Cannery, that parking lot near Ghirardelli Square, a restaurant at Pier 1, and an apartment building a few blocks up the street. The Sea Gull Arms, I think he said."

Ed groaned. "Oh, no, that's where I live!"

"And that's just what he owns on this street, Wynn," Lula said sadly. "God only knows what he owns in the rest of the city—or the state—the country, for that matter!"

Wynn cried out in exasperation, "So what! Who cares? I've never heard you carry on this way about the financial situation of any other client. In fact, I've seen you send us wives out to people you never even billed, because you knew they couldn't pay the going rate! In fact, it's that kind of business practice that's helped get you where you are today! So why should this client's money be so important?"

Lula shook her head and smiled dismally. "No, no, Wynn, you've got it all wrong, dear. A. J. Stone isn't a client. He's a financier, a backer, an angel—if you'll pardon the expression. He's the one I was counting on to lend us enough money to keep Helpmates from going under. He could've kept us afloat for another year at least. But now, I guess, we're sunk."

That night Wynn was the victim of a ferocious attack of insomnia. Her brain felt like a frustrated laboratory mouse trying to make its way through a maze. Finally at three o'clock in the morning she turned on the bedside lamp and sat up in her rumpled bed, knowing it was useless to try to sleep.

How on earth had she landed in such a muddled mess? she thought distractedly. Just because some judgmental, vindictive man had come to the bizarre conclusion that she was a woman of easy virtue—a call girl, of all things!— she was now the cause of Lula's losing the backing that would have bought another year of grace for her fledgling business.

And, adding insult to injury, there was also her own shocking response to that terrible man's sinister charisma. Now, sitting up in bed, her elbows propped on raised knees, Wynn held her flushed cheeks and aching head in her hands. Conflicting thoughts raced around in her mind and collided like the blips on the screen of a video war game. How could a rational, sensible person like herself have responded so giddily to that rude, overbearing stranger? She didn't even like his type—that arrogant manner, so common in the physically favored man—that elegant machismo, born of wealth and power. Why couldn't a sweet, kind man like Ed Patterson evoke that rush of desire in her blood, that liquid feeling in her bones? It was so unfair!

Never mind that now, she commanded herself. With a great effort she closed her mind to the memory of his marauding kiss, the scent of his breath as he nuzzled her neck, that knowing look in his sable brown eyes. Punching her pillow in futile anger, she told herself that was all irrelevant to the real problem at hand.

What she had to do now was restore the integrity of Lula's business in the eyes of that fanatical, puritanical Scrooge. She had to convince Aaron Stone that Lula's business was a good investment, a legitimate, ethical business filling the serious needs of modern people—and not a front for some dubious, shady operation, as he seemed to think it was.

But how?

CHAPTER FIVE

After a few hours of fitful sleep, Wynn decided, not being of a devious nature, that her only chance lay in simply bearding the lion in his den, stating her case honestly, and hoping for the best. To that end, she'd called Sherri at Helpmates and asked her for Aaron Stone's phone number. Wynn sat now in her pretty red and white kitchen, nibbling her fingernails, and looking in dread from the slip of paper with his number on it to the red phone hanging on her kitchen wall. Finally, with a last deep breath to steady herself, she dialed the number and with unbelievable speed was put through to the great man himself.

"Stone here," he said abruptly.

Unthinkingly Wynn murmured, "Too true."

"What's that? Please speak up," he ordered.

With a shudder that he might've have heard her, Wynn said quickly, "Mr. Stone, this is Wynn Harris from Helpmates." When there was no reply but a menacing silence on the line, Wynn added nervously, "We met . . . ah, recently?"

"Yes, I remember it well," he drawled. "So you've called me after all."

"Pardon?" Wynn said, confused.

"I told you not to call me—that I'd call you. What's the matter? Is business so slow?" he quipped lightly.

In spite of the fact that there was no particular hostility in his tone, Wynn felt a rush of adrenaline, and with the rashness of anger she retorted coldly, "Mr. Stone, I called on Lula Dobbs's account, because I felt I must, not because I wanted to. But not even for Lula will I take any more insults from you. So good-bye." Wynn hung up the receiver with a satisfying crash.

Her heart jumped when within seconds the phone rang. She stared at it for a few rings, marshaling several devastating one-liners, then snatched it up and mimicking his own cold, abrupt manner, she said, "Harris here."

"Wynn, don't be childish, don't hang up again," Aaron said urgently. Then when he heard no reply but silence on the line, he continued smoothly. "You said you wanted to talk about Ms. Dobbs. The only time I can give you is at lunch. But that should suit you very well, accustomed as you are to mixing business with pleasure."

Wynn admitted a begrudging admiration for his style. What a barracuda he must be in a business deal. All in one breath he insulted her again, made no apology for the last insult, but instead shifted the blame from himself to her by calling her justified reaction childish, while at the same time acceding to her request to speak to him about Lula. Wynn's sleep-starved mind, befuddled by his masterly manipulation, took refuge in the emotional as she said defiantly, "I don't want to have lunch with you, Mr. Stone. I'd have to be a masochist to find pleasure in your company."

"Oh? That's odd. That's not the impression I got Saturday night." Wynn could sense the smug smile on his face.

Her denial came quickly. "You're entirely mistaken, I assure you!"

After a pause just long enough to establish his disbelief, Aaron said, "As you wish. But be that as it may, the lunch hour really is the only available time I have today." Then he added sarcastically, "Perhaps it won't offend your sensibilities too much if you simply sit at the table with me while I eat."

Wynn hesitated, then agreed in a sulky tone. "Oh, all right, but only because you give me no choice."

"That's a good girl. My office is on the top floor of the Standard Building. Meet me there at noon. Oh, and, Wynn, please note that I kept my word—I did call you." And with that he hung up before Wynn could beat him to it.

His last jibe was somewhat buffered for Wynn by the news that his office and Helpmates, Inc., shared a building. She couldn't recall ever seeing his name on the directory at the elevators, although his business might be called anything, and she'd never paid much attention to the directory anyway.

As Wynn showered, washed her hair, and blow-dried it, her mind restlessly played back the recent conversation. The more she dwelled on it the angrier and more worried she became. Now that the first hurdle was passed, that of gaining his ear, the important one still loomed ahead. If it weren't for Lula, Wynn could have chalked this whole ridiculous farce up to experience and forgotten it. After all! What did she care if one sour, suspicious man had some twisted opinion of her in his tiny, sick mind? But there *was* Lula, and somehow Wynn had to convince him.

She peered into her closet, anxiously thinking what people in the most serious professions wore. The clergy— black. Judges—black. Morticians—surely black! And doctors—white. Of course. Black and white. A combination so dignified and sober that even Aaron Stone couldn't see it as frivolous or provocative.

A short while later Wynn scrutinized her appearance in the full-length mirror. Thank heaven she'd recently bought this black lightweight wool suit at Joseph Magnin's. Even on sale it had cost an arm and a leg, but because of its classical design Wynn had considered it an investment. The four-gored skirt hung gracefully, and under the well-fitting open jacket she wore a silk blouse in

57

a small diamond pattern with a soft full bow at the neck-line. Her hose were gunmetal gray and her shoes were simple black leather pumps.

She wore her glossy black hair pulled back into a chignon, the way she'd worn it on that evil night she'd met Aaron Stone. Even though her hairstyle hadn't seemed to go far toward convincing him of her virtue that night, it was still the most dignified and respectable style she knew of. In fact, it was downright austere. For jewelry she wore only a pair of medium-sized gold dome earrings, and her makeup was applied with a sparing hand. Yes, Wynn thought, she looked the very soul of chastity and rectitude. In fact, maybe even dull and boring. In short—perfect.

When Wynn arrived at the Standard Building, she hoped she wouldn't run into anyone from Helpmates, especially Lula, who probably would not want Wynn to ask any favors of the man who'd cast aspersions on her business. As she waited anxiously for the elevator she found Stone & Assoc., Inc., on the building directory. The queasiness in Wynn's stomach was too pronounced to be blamed on the elevator alone as it swept her up to the meeting she dreaded.

When she stepped out, the first thing she noticed was that Stone & Assoc., Inc., seemed to occupy the entire floor. The second thing she noticed was A. J. Stone himself. He negligently half-sat on the corner of the vacated receptionist's desk, bracing himself with one long leg outstretched before him. As he watched Wynn approach, his face was an expressionless mask, but Wynn detected a scary speculative glint in his dark eyes. When she stopped a safe six feet from him, he glanced pointedly down at his wrist watch. "You're late," he commented.

Flushing with pique, Wynn too glanced at her watch which, thank God, was actually on her wrist this time. "Your watch is wrong, I believe," she countered airily, determined to give as good as she got from this bully.

Aaron stood up and advanced toward her. "My watch is never wrong. Come along now." He grasped her by the elbow and turned her around to once again approach the elevator. Wynn found it objectionable to be grasped and steered about like a grocery cart, but she felt this was not the time to make her protests known. And as soon as the doors whispered shut, trapping her in the small space with him, her heart began to bang against her ribs. Then when she saw him take a funny-looking key from his pocket and insert it in an equally funny-looking aperture on the floor-button panel, her anxiety rose to new heights.

"What are you doing?" she demanded.

Aaron looked down at her as if she might be a refugee just arrived from some remote, underdeveloped country. "I'm unlocking the elevator so we can go up to the penthouse where we will have lunch."

Disgruntled, Wynn muttered, "Oh. I wasn't aware that there was a restaurant in the building."

Wynn was just thinking how odd it was that in the year she'd worked here she'd never heard of a restaurant, when it came to her in a flash that it was highly unlikely a restaurant would be hidden away behind lock and key. Before she could think what to do, Aaron again took hold of her and steered her out of the elevator and toward a very beautifully grained wooden door—a blank door.

"Now just a minute," she said, pulling back. "This is no restaurant. Is it?"

Aaron left her standing in the middle of the hall as he unlocked the door and pushed it open. "No, it is not. I never said it was. This is where I live. Won't you come in?" And then he grinned evilly at her and added, " 'Said the spider to the fly.' "

In spite of her alarmed state, or perhaps because of it, Wynn laughed nervously at his obviously mock menace. Making no attempt to touch her now, Aaron stood relaxed in the open doorway smiling with amusement, an expression that quite transformed his handsome, but until now, dour, brooding face. This entirely new aspect of his personality fascinated Wynn, and she felt her rigid caution ease just a bit.

In an attempt to recover her poise and at the same time reestablish the fact that this was a business meeting, Wynn cocked her head to one side and said wryly as she stepped through the door, "If you pay rent here for an apartment as well as for your business, you surely understand one reason why Lula needs a loan."

Aaron's muffled reply was lost to Wynn as she gradually became aware of her surroundings. At first she saw only that the apartment was a masterpiece of modern architectural design. From the immense foyer where she stood Wynn could see the huge sunken living area. The glass walls on three sides of the room offered a panoramic view of the Bay Bridge to the east, the Golden Gate Bridge to the west, and, toward the north, the lush green of Marin County nestled at the base of Mt. Tamalpais. At night one would be surrounded by the festive glitter of the entire city's lights.

When the spare, ultra-modern grandeur of the room itself faded into the background of Wynn's consciousness, she began to notice the sharp contrast of the furnishings that dotted the vast expanse of gray velvet carpet. She guessed that not one piece had been manufactured after 1920 and even then had been designed more for endurance than style. The furniture was not arranged in any way that might invite human congeniality but instead seemed abandoned, like weary travelers stranded in an empty bus station late at night. The woods were grimly dark and the upholstery colors brackish. The whole ambience of the room was that of a beaten, resigned one—an appalling, sad room.

Wynn asked herself why a man rich enough to both live here and pay commercial rent for an entire floor of the building, who dressed in such expensive clothes with such impeccable taste, would live in such dismal, shabby surroundings. Aaron may have seen the look of puzzlement on her face, for as he took her arm to guide her to the dining room, he remarked too casually, "I haven't had time to do much with the place, as you see."

When Wynn murmured in agreement, he added a bit defensively, "And I've just recently lost my housekeeper." As if, Wynn thought, any housekeeper could have made a dent in this pitiful room's problems.

The dining room table was dark and massive, with ugly bulbous knobs on its trunklike legs. Resting on its worn surface were two gorgeous silver salvers with domed tops from which the aroma of good food wafted into the air. The table was set with creamy china banded in gold, silver flatware with an old-fashioned intricate design, and sparkling etched crystal. The linen napkins, although mended with delicate stitches, were velvety smooth and supple with age. There was a charming centerpiece of blushing pears amid glossy green citrus leaves. Wynn felt oddly relieved at these signs of sumptuousness and tradition, as if they proved that her dining companion was not altogether indifferent to the pleasures of the senses, after all. As Aaron guided her by the elbow to seat her at the table, Wynn repressed an involuntary shiver at the now gentle, almost caressing touch of his hand.

"How very lovely the table looks," she said to break the awkward silence. "Do you lunch so elegantly every day?"

Aaron too now looked over the table, but with an inspector's eye. "No, I'm trying out the services of a new caterer today. Thought I'd kill two birds with one stone." He looked at Wynn expectantly and out of reflex politeness she smiled weakly at his morbid pun.

Then, pouring Wynn a glass of wine the color of pale topaz, Aaron asked, "And do you always dress so provocatively at lunch?"

Taken aback, Wynn looked down at her clothing in alarm while her right hand nervously smoothed at her hair. "But I'm not!"

Still standing, Aaron leaned over and ran his palm over the smooth black helmet of Wynn's hair, then brushed the back of his fingers against her cheek. "But you are. When a woman wears her hair all pinned up like that, the first thing a man thinks of is pulling out the pins and watching it tumble down over bare shoulders."

Wynn stared at him with wide, startled eyes. "Really, you're wrong!" she protested vehemently.

"No, I am not wrong. That's exactly what I'm thinking," he said firmly.

"No, no, I mean I didn't intend—"

"And those clothes," he said, sitting down and lifting the cover from one of the trays. "So purposely cold and severe that one is forced to imagine the warm delights that lie beneath."

Wynn's cheeks, still tingling from the touch of his hand, now stung with color. "Mr. Stone, I'll thank you to stop making such . . . personal remarks! *Now* who's mixing business with pleasure?" she said, pleased that she'd scored a point for once.

But Aaron merely nodded, smiling with self-satisfaction. "I thought that remark would please you. I'm just surprised you admit it."

Speechless with indignation and confusion, Wynn watched him place before her a plate of Persian melon draped with succulent pink prosciutto. Fixing on something concrete to object to, she said haughtily, "Thank you, no. If you'll remember, I agreed only to sit at the table with you while you ate."

Aaron picked up his fork. "If you actually want to be that childish . . ." he shrugged eloquently.

Completely discomfited, Wynn was forced by pride now to sit rigidly at the table like some naughty child at boarding school and watch the headmaster eat. Once or twice she did take a quick sip of her wine, not knowing what else to do, but afraid to say a word for fear he'd somehow turn it against her again, she waited quietly while he finished the first course.

Wynn thought it was the hardest thing she'd ever done. One couldn't stare at someone while he ate—and yet how sullen it would look to stare down at the plate in front of her. Nor could one gape about the room like a provincial fool, and, besides, there was nothing in the room worth looking at.

In defense from her acute embarrassment, Wynn's mind began to offer her wild but interesting things to think about. Did he really mean what he'd said about her bare shoulders? If so, why wasn't she affronted instead of secretly pleased and flattered, just as he'd said, damn him. And how had he called her back so swiftly this morning if he hadn't previously found out her phone number? And if he had—why? Did he really think what he professed to think of her? If so, why should he have taken the trouble to follow her home Saturday night, to bring her the coat and handbag she'd left behind in her panic? But if he didn't think she was . . . well, easy, then why did he pretend to think it? And most of all, Wynn thought of that kiss.

From under her eyelashes, she surreptitiously studied those wide, firm lips now moving so slightly as he chewed his food. She noticed again the lean jaws that sloped so elegantly toward the strong chin that had once nestled in the hollow of her shoulder. And she wondered at the mysterious, faraway expression in those compelling dark eyes. All this Wynn saw before she lowered her gaze to the safety of the napkin spread uselessly open on her sensible black wool skirt.

She jumped when he suddenly said, "I can tell from the

hungry look on your face that you're having second thoughts about refusing lunch, Wynn."

A blush flamed over her face. If her expression was so transparent, thank heaven he couldn't actually read her mind.

"Let's call a halt to this stubborn foolishness now, shall we? I really must insist that you try the next course and give me your honest opinion." He removed her untouched food and took the plates to a hulking sideboard against the far wall. Then he lifted the cover of the second salver to reveal six small oval quenelles gently bathed in a velvety velouté sauce. Beside them in a silver dish were lovely bright green *petit pois*. With a sigh of mixed resignation and relief, Wynn allowed Aaron to save her from her own pride. Without a hint of protest, she accepted the divine-looking food he placed before her, for in truth she was faint with hunger.

"As you no doubt know," he began pedantically, "a well-made quenelle is one of the acid tests when judging a new cook."

The morsel of ground fish and pastry, poached in broth, felt as light as a soufflé on Wynn's tongue. "Mmmm," she murmured, nodding her approval. "Are you thinking of hiring this caterer for a party, then?" she asked conversationally.

Aaron carefully inspected the texture of the sauce as he absently answered, "Yes, I suppose I'll use them myself—if I decide to buy the company. Or maybe even if I don't. These quenelle are really first-rate, don't you agree?"

Wynn lowered her fork from her mouth. "Do you mean to say that you're testing their cooking because you may buy the company?" she asked carefully.

Aaron looked up at her with a questioning smile. "Isn't that what I just said? Is it so odd to sample wares before one buys them?"

He'd said he was killing two birds with one stone, Wynn

thought excitedly. For the first time, she had a real hope that her foray into the eagle's eyrie might actually bear fruit. "No, of course not. It's very prudent. But surely you don't make your decisions based on just one performance? What else do you do before deciding to buy—or invest in—a company?" she asked with vital interest.

"I study the books, of course. I look at the list of clients, if that's applicable. I check into the owner's background, and I meet with the key personnel. And then, after I test the product, I go with my instincts."

Wynn idly pushed a tiny pea to the center of her plate, then inquired casually, "And how much of that had you done with Helpmates before—"

"Don't forget, I was only considering making Ms. Dobbs a loan, not buying into her business," he interrupted. "But to answer your question, I'd looked into her background and scanned her books. That's as far as I'd gotten when I saw you plying your trade in public on Sunday afternoon. From there I went directly to instinct."

"Well, in this case your instincts were all wrong!" Wynn retorted before she could restrain the geyser of anger Aaron Stone's words evoked. She struggled to control herself; there was entirely too much at stake for her react to his insults, now that she'd made a little progress. But her voice quavered with hurt as she added more calmly, "And on the basis of that one utterly erroneous assumption, you decided not to help her."

"No, not at all," Aaron replied. "Erroneous or not, I based my assumption on two events—not one. Surely you can't have forgotten dear old Buckie Packard? That, added to Ms. Dobbs's weak background in business and the pitiable state of her finances, clinched the matter. I felt it would be kinder to let the business die a natural death rather than employ heroic lifesaving measures." He added wryly, "Especially with my money."

"What do you mean, weak business background? Lula

worked in her husband's dry goods business for thirty years! She's a smart, hardworking woman. She has vision!" Wynn defended her boss hotly.

Aaron's smile was condescending. "She may be a fine, plucky little woman—I'm sure she is. And she may know merchandising. But she doesn't know service. She runs that hobby of hers with all the business acumen of a suburban garage sale."

"Well, she's still learning! The business is just a year old—and it's a new concept!"

Aaron laughed. "A new concept? It's the oldest concept in the world just dressed up in trendy new clothes."

"Oh!" Wynn gasped. "You really are unbelievable. I don't even know why I'm wasting my time with a Neanderthal like you."

She pushed back her chair and prepared to rise, but Aaron reached over and took hold of her arm, plunking her back in her chair. Fixing a steely eye on her until he was sure she'd stay put, he drawled, "My, my, such righteousness. If you don't calm down, I'll think the lady doth protest too much." Then, with élan, he broke off a bit of a Parker House roll and dabbed it in the sauce on his empty plate. "All right, let's assume—just for the moment, and just for the sake of argument—that Helpmates is actually a legitimate business. Then I'd say to you that it's a ridiculous, insane idea that will never work. What are we coming to, I'd like to know, when some woman thinks she can build a business out of selling various and sundry personal services that anyone can get free from family and friends?"

Wynn tried to interject, "You're wrong, Aaron. You don't understand—"

But Aaron overrode her attempt. "And calling her employees wives—that's pure California hype—pure glitz. What next! Rent-a-friend? Rent-a-foe? How about Rent-a-child—now there's a business that would fly today. And, of course, that good old standby with a catchy new name —Rent-a-lover."

"Aaron, if you'll just let me give you a few statistics—"

"And then there's that ridiculous motto: We can give you anything but love," he scoffed. "That's the code phrase that gives your real intention away. Haven't you heard of Newspeak? Haven't you read *1984*? 'War Is Peace.' 'Freedom Is Slavery.' 'Ignorance Is Strength.' When you say you *don't* give love, the real message is that you *do* give love. Love—the euphemism of the century for cheap intimacy—in short, for sex."

Aaron fell silent, avoiding Wynn's eyes, a brooding frown on his face. Appalled at his bizarre flight of fancy, Wynn saw now that her task was even more difficult than she'd thought, and she wondered if Lula wasn't better off without his help. Still, since she'd come this far . . .

"You're not only crazy, Aaron Stone, you're paranoid as well," Wynn said hotly. "Now, maybe you haven't noticed it here in your ivory tower, but this isn't 1950 anymore. Today about fifty-two percent of all women between the ages of nineteen and fifty-nine are employed outside the home. That's nationally. I'd guess it's even higher in the cities. Nearly forty percent of all women over forty work. Mama isn't home anymore and neither is Grandma. *And Daddy never was.*"

Wynn thought for a second she'd seen Aaron wince, but she ignored it. She'd had to listen to him rant—now let him listen to her! "Today only eleven percent of all American families still fit the mold of the traditional nuclear family with father at work and mother at home with the kids. And the number of single-parent households is growing by leaps and bounds.

"I suppose I ought to point out to a man like you who doesn't know how the other half lives that these people are

67

working out of the necessity to support their families; they can't afford full-time help like you can. So, now you tell me: if Mama is out working to help support the family, and so are most of her friends, and so is her mother—where is she going to find those helpful friends and family to do little favors for her that you speak of so confidently? Who will wait at home all day for the washer repairman? Who will run around in a car all day grocery shopping and taking Daddy's suits to the cleaners and the dog to the vet? There are only so many hours in a day, you know. When she comes home from work there are still children to be raised, meals to cook, laundry to wash—a life to live! Helpmates is needed, and people are grateful for our services! If you looked at our books, you should've seen how heavy our cash flow is—"

Aaron interjected, "But Ms. Dobbs catches the flow in a sieve instead of a bucket."

Wynn made a wide, dismissing gesture. "Now you're talking business practice, not legitimacy. And that brings me to your last insane remark, Mr. Stone."

Aaron sat listening to her with a closed, stubborn look on his face as Wynn began to explain that the wives at Helpmates sold their time, their skills, their judgment, and their physical labor.

"Nobody, but nobody, sells his or her affections, Mr. Stone, either physically or emotionally. I admit that people do sell their bodies in this world, and since you seem to have it on the brain, you're obviously acutely aware of that fact too. But *not* at Helpmates! As for affection, it can't be bought or sold, neither within marriage nor outside it. By its very nature affection can only be freely given. It is truly a favor and truly priceless—that is, without price."

"Yes," Aaron said shortly, "I remember well your telling me once before how priceless your favors are."

Wynn's shoulders slumped in defeat. Obviously this perverse creature was determined to think the worst of her. Her voice was quiet as she wearily replied, "You said that, not I. I said you hadn't enough money to buy my favors, but you know I was using the word in *your* context. And you forced me to it anyway. You insulted me and I struck back. It's as simple as that."

"So you say now," Aaron said tightly. "And you say it very touchingly. But all the same, the two times I've seen you using this skill and judgment you speak of, once you were in the company of a shabby man, his accomplice in a shabby enterprise, and the second time you were behaving in a loose and vulgar manner in public. I fail to see why either of these examples of your *work* should inspire me with confidence in Ms. Dobbs's business."

"No, I don't see why either, Mr. Stone. And I can't imagine why I ever thought if I came here I could convince you that you'd made a mistake, that Helpmates is an ethical, much-needed modern service, and that it deserves a helping hand.

"But you're right. Oh, I suppose I could tell you that the first time you saw me I was the one sinned against, not the sinner. And I could tell you that the second time I was freely expressing my affection for a friend, and publicly or not, I think that can't be vulgar. But I see now it would take a miracle for you to simply extend me the ordinary human courtesy of believing I speak the truth. And we both know that miracles never happen, don't we."

Wynn rose from the table and this time Aaron didn't try to stop her. As she walked out of the dining room and through the dreary living area she could feel him following behind her. When she reached the foyer she turned to confront him.

"Thank you for giving me a little of your time, Mr. Stone. It's been an education. I've never before met a person as suspicious and wrong-headed and negative as you are."

The first instant of surprise was quickly camouflaged with a sardonic smile. "Well, you're young yet; you'll meet others of us sooner or later. There are plenty of us skulking around in the world," he said caustically.

At this retort, at his show of invulnerability, Wynn felt a terrible urge to hurt him, to wipe that smile from his face. "You must have a very sad and lonely life. Do you have a pet to keep you company? Something to suit your personality—like a wolverine or a ferret perhaps?"

When Aaron's dark thick eyebrows rose high in amazement, Wynn took a nervous step backward, expecting an explosion of anger. But, incredibly, he began to laugh. Wynn stood transfixed as he fell weakly against the wall, then ricocheted up right again, the gales of laughter erupting from the strong column of his throat to boom against the marble of the foyer.

Stepping toward her, he gathered Wynn in his arms and still he laughed, making her fear for her eardrums. Alarmed at his completely unexpected reaction, Wynn hung in his grasp as motionless as a rabbit in the jaws of a jackal. What madness was he up to now? she wondered bitterly. Oh, how she resented his power to keep her emotions on a roller coaster from the first moment she'd met him!

As the intimate pressure of his body warmed the length of hers, Wynn tried desperately to fix on the anger she'd felt toward him just seconds ago, but there was no denying the eager swell of her breasts against his hard, broad chest. A soft gust of his laughter blew warm against her neck, and the reverberations of his mirth traveled to her very core. Again the aroma of spicy almond delighted her nostrils, and Wynn's body responded with a ripple of desire.

"Oh, God," Aaron gasped at last, "what have I done to deserve this? You really are priceless."

His words returned Wynn to reality and she pushed against his chest. "Let me go," she insisted, her voice muffled in his jacket.

With a final, groaning chuckle and a heavy, satisfied sigh, Aaron loosed one arm from Wynn's shoulders to put his hand in his pocket. He handed her a key ring with two keys on it.

"What's this?" she asked suspiciously.

"This is for you to come in here on Friday and start preparing for a dinner party for Saturday night. If you do it to my satisfaction, I'll reconsider making a loan to Helpmates."

Wynn looked at him askance. Was this another one of his sick jokes? "You will?" she asked dubiously.

"Of course. Why not? Did you ever doubt it?" He smiled down at the skeptical astonishment in her face. "I'll call you on Wednesday and give you the details. But now I'm afraid I must get back to work."

Wynn's burgeoning joy at this unexpected outcome was barely born when it began to die. She couldn't do it this weekend! That was her standing appointment with Ed and his kids. For agonizing seconds Wynn wavered, frowning. At her hesitation Aaron's face took on a stormy look, rattling her further.

"Well?" he demanded. "Will you do it or won't you?"

Fearfully she stammered, "It's just that I have a previous job booked next weekend . . ."

"Get someone else to substitute for you!"

"I could, I suppose . . . but—"

"But what? Is it another one of your specialties—mixing business with pleasure? Is that it?" he said, his voice taking on that hardness she'd grown to dread.

"No, no, of course not," Wynn fibbed, asking forgiveness in her heart for her betrayal of poor Ed and the children. "I was just thinking it would be easier to get another wife for you," she rushed on. "Someone who cooks much better than I," she offered hopefully.

Aaron's eyes grew cool. "You asked for a chance to prove you're a competent employee of a legitimate business, didn't you? So, either you take the assignment yourself or the whole deal is off." Then, in a dangerously silky tone, he added, "After all, you're the only wife who's under suspicion, aren't you?"

CHAPTER SIX

Because of Aaron's highhandedness, Wynn was forced to rearrange her entire week. As he'd said he would, he'd called on Wednesday morning and given her "the details."

"I'll leave the menu up to you," he said graciously, "as long as you don't serve any of that funky ethnic food so pervasive in San Francisco."

Wynn sighed. She hadn't even begun and already he was being difficult. "If you mean Chinese or Japanese, I can't cook them anyway."

"They're not ethnic. You know what I mean—cuisine from countries nobody ever heard of until last week."

"How about prime ribs and Yorkshire pudding," Wynn suggested wryly. "England has been around awhile."

"Excellent. There's nothing better than plain food if it's properly prepared."

The memory of him feeding her that succulent piece of beef Wellington the night she'd met him flashed into her mind and she lost the beginning of his next remark.

". . . the place festive."

"Festive? Did you say make your apartment festive?" she asked, alarmed that he expected a miracle.

After a second's silence he replied defensively, "Maybe not festive, exactly . . . but pleasant at least." Then impatiently, "You're supposed to do for me what a wife would do, aren't you? Then do as you please. Either I'll like it or I won't. That's the agreement, isn't it?"

Therefore, sparing no expense, Wynn ordered flowers and groceries from shops that catered to the carriage trade to be delivered on Friday when she'd spend the day trying to make Aaron's warehouselike residence look habitable, if not festive.

With great reluctance Wynn broached Ed with the news of her defection on the coming weekend. Expecting his disappointment and protests, she was surprised when he took it so well. Half relieved and half chagrined, Wynn wondered if his reaction was due to understanding the importance of Wynn's new assignment to Lula's business or to the fact that Lula's pretty granddaughter, Meg, agreed to fill in for her.

She'd also had to change her Friday evening appointment with Professor Jenkins to another evening, knowing she'd be too tired to give him his due after a day wrestling with what she now thought of as an impossible and ill-conceived task. Wynn despaired of ever pleasing Aaron enough to make him change his mind about Helpmates. Even if he'd been a less demanding person than he obviously was, Wynn realized that something about this whole comedy of errors caused a reaction that, even for him, was out of proportion. *There are none so blind as those who will not see,* Wynn thought morosely.

It was in this depressed mood that Wynn remained the entire evening as she read the last numbing chapter of *Madame Bovary* to Professor Jenkins. When she'd finished reading that last bitterly ironic sentence and closed the book, her eyes were filled with tears and her heart ached in her breast. "Oh, poor Charles," Wynn quavered, wiping at her eyes with the knuckles of one hand.

"My dear child," Professor Jenkins murmured in concern, "remember, it's only a novel. Perhaps the greatest novel ever written, but only fiction, nevertheless." From the pocket in his green wool cardigan sweater, he took a clean handkerchief and offered it to Wynn. "Does Emma's husband seem the victim of the book to you, then, rather than Emma herself?"

Wynn sighed deeply, trying to compose herself. "Well, it's strange. When I first read the book I was fourteen years old. Then, I wept—sobbed, if you want the truth—for Emma. I saw her as a romantic trapped in dull domesticity, caged in marriage to a mediocre, small-minded man." Wynn glanced at the professor with a watery smile. "I saw the handsome, charming Rodolphe and his wealth and background as a goal worth dying for. Now I see him as the selfish villain he is," Wynn said intensely. "I must have been a very stupid child to have ever thought differently."

"Oh, I think not," the professor said, serving their customary post-reading refreshment. "Part of the book's greatness—any book, for that matter—lies in its power to make us see ourselves in the characters. And symbolically speaking, all of us, I believe, have buried hopes that the prince will someday come and kiss the sleeping princess back to life."

Wynn smiled wryly as she sipped her tea.

"You disagree?" the professor asked gently. "Don't forget, even the cynical Flaubert himself, who set out to write a book damning bourgeois romanticism and sentimentality, said of his character, 'Madame Bovary, c'est moi'—it's me."

"Well, perhaps I just know too much about princes to believe in them anymore," Wynn said ironically.

"Ah? What an intriguing remark." The professor settled back in his armchair. "Will you tell me about the princes you've known?"

Wynn too sagged back into her chair, wrung out from the overdose of emotionality she'd experienced the past week. As if it weren't bad enough that her mind had obsessively worried about Aaron Stone, she'd also been unable to stop ruminating about the father she'd never known—something she seldom did. She looked over at the wise, weathered face of her companion and saw in it an interest born of gentle affection. It suddenly occurred to Wynn that of all the hundreds of people she knew, there was no one in whom she'd ever felt comfortable confiding the facts of her past. But now she could feel that desire, that need, welling up in her, too strong to be denied.

"My father was a prince, I suppose," she began tersely, "a black Irish prince." She laughed shortly. "A black sheep, at any rate. He came from a wealthy eastern mining family, but in his adolescence he rebelled against his background and ran off to become a jazz musician."

"It doesn't sound too wicked so far," Professor Jenkins interjected softly. "Romantic, if anything,"

Wynn smiled to acknowledge his effort to help her keep a possibly painful recital on the level of a fairy tale. "It gets worse," she promised. "When he was in his mid-twenties he came through the little town in the Midwest where my mother lived with her family. They were very respectable people. Pillars of the community, I suppose one would say. My grandfather taught art history at a small liberal arts college there and my grandmother was president of the ladies' garden club and the organist of her church choir. Are you getting the picture?" Wynn asked.

"Indeed I am. You're describing my very own world, Wynn, until my dear wife passed away and I moved to the city."

"Maybe so, but I know you'd never have reacted as my grandparents did to what happened next. My mother was very young, just out of high school, when my father came to town. And, oh, she was so beautiful, Professor," Wynn said fervently, her gaze turned inward to the tale she'd begged to hear again and again, as a child. "She wanted desperately to hear the jazz group—I think only because it was something different to do in that small town—but she knew her parents would forbid it. They were playing at a roadhouse on the edge of town, you see, that was strictly off limits to nice girls."

The professor nodded knowingly and refilled Wynn's cup with fresh, hot tea. Absentmindedly, she took a swallow before she continued. "So she told them a fib and went with a group of her friends. You can guess what came next, can't you?" Wynn smiled with chagrin. "She fell madly in love with him at first sight. And, he with her, too, for a while, at least. He was in town only a few days, but it was long enough to ruin three lives."

"He . . . ah, loved her and left her . . . in the family way?" the professor suggested with old-world delicacy.

Wynn shook her head. "No, not then, anyway. Maybe if he had, she'd have been better off. But no, my mother tried to play the game according to the rules of the day. She took my father home to meet her parents, she announced that they were in love—he even asked my grandfather for her hand in marriage!" Wynn laughed with sharp bitterness. "Of course, my grandfather denied them permission to marry. Can't you just see it," Wynn asked sardonically, "this innocent, country girl just out of high school and this slick, jaded jazz musician on his way to Chicago and the big time?"

"So she eloped with him," the professor said.

"Yes," Wynn replied dully. "He detoured to Tennessee where a seventeen-year-old girl could legally marry without her parents' permission. She traveled with him during the next year while his band toured the country, never staying in one place for more than a weekend. They were in San Francisco when she realized she was pregnant. She was just eighteen years old."

Wynn fell silent, swallowing with difficulty. The professor sat quietly, waiting for her to finish her story. When she at last raised her eyes to his, they shimmered with unshed tears. "When my mother got to this part of the story, she always phrased it to show how *good* her hus-

77

band was to her," Wynn said with bitterness. "When she told him she was pregnant, he explained to her that his career wasn't suited to domesticity or fatherhood. Somehow he raised the money to put a down payment on a small house in a newly developed section of the city. He said he'd send her money regularly, told her he loved her, and left her there in an alien city, estranged from her family, pregnant, and eighteen years old. She never heard from him again. Twelve years later she got a letter from a member of the old band, telling her he'd died of a heart attack in New Orleans."

"Oh, my dear child, I'm so sorry," said the professor in a voice husky with sympathy. "And she never turned to her family for help?"

"She tried to patch things up that year they were traveling. She wrote regular letters, and from time to time she'd call them long distance. But the letters were never answered and my grandfather was unfailingly cold on the phone. He wouldn't even let her speak to my grandmother. And even after I was born"—Wynn's voice broke and the hot tears fell now—"they never forgave her."

"My dear girl, what can I say to you?" the professor asked helplessly. "She must have been very bitter, to lose so much because of your father."

With a shuddering sigh Wynn shook her head. "But she wasn't. At least, if she was, she never let me see it. She always said that year with him was worth whatever price she'd had to pay for it. And I think, now, she took great care that I should never feel I was the cause of him leaving her because she said over and over that having me was like having the best part of him with her always."

The professor's expression was thoughtful. "Wynn, I believe your mother was one of those lucky few who have stolen a touch of heaven." At Wynn's puzzled look, the professor explained. "She reminds me of a quote from a French writer, Madame de Giradin, who said, 'To love one who loves you, to admire one who admires you, in a word, to be the idol of one's idol, is exceeding the limit of human joy; it is stealing fire from heaven.' And even if that love between them lasted just a year, Wynn, it was more than many people have in a lifetime."

"Maybe you're right, Professor," Wynn said tiredly. "She was a wonderful woman, that much I know. I miss her dreadfully. Every day of our lives together she tried to make me see my father as she saw him. But as I grew up and began to understand the implications of what he'd done to her—and to me—it was I who grew bitter. It was I who was never able to forgive him," Wynn confessed.

The professor smiled and gently inquired, "And now there's another prince in your life whom you also can't forgive?"

Wynn blushed deeply. "No, Professor. Well, there is but it's purely business. He may be a prince—a merchant prince—but he's certainly not my prince. I wouldn't have him, or anyone like him, on a silver platter. Give me a nice, quiet, ordinary man, any day!"

The professor busied himself with the tea tray, his back turned to Wynn as he commented casually, "I wonder, Wynn, is it possible to suffer from Bovaryism in reverse? That is, to romanticize the ordinary man and despise the extraordinary? Can it really be true that every quiet, plodding, ordinary man must make a loving, faithful husband? And every wealthy, worldly, handsome man must be a treacherous, selfish, arrogant bounder?"

Then, to take any possible sting out of his remarks, the professor turned to Wynn, smiling, and said playfully, "On the other hand, I myself seem to prove your point, Wynn. There could be no more quiet, plodding, ordinary man than I and yet, if you'll pardon my immodesty, I was a faithful and loving husband for twenty-five years, and long to be so again, if I could find a woman as right for me as my dear wife was. She and I were among those lucky few who stole a touch of heaven, like your mother."

Wynn contemplated the older man's kind, gentle face. "How I wish my mother could have known you, Professor."

"I wish it too, Wynn. I think I would've liked her very much indeed."

With a deep blush, Wynn murmured, "And I wish I'd had a father like you."

The professor crossed to Wynn's chair and leaned down to kiss her on the brow. "Thank you, my dear. That's a very fine compliment, coming from a young woman like you. But if I'm not privileged to be your father, I will certainly be your loving friend."

CHAPTER SEVEN

Wynn arrived at Aaron's penthouse about nine o'clock the following Friday morning. She'd deliberately delayed her arrival to ensure that he'd have left for the office, but even so she rang the doorbell. When there was no answer from within, she cautiously unlocked the massive door with the key he'd given her and stepped gingerly into the foyer. She stood motionless, like a doe in the forest listening for sounds of the hunter. Hearing nothing but the eerie silence of empty space, she relaxed and closed the door behind her.

The first thing she saw as she entered the morose living area was a beautiful full-length white satin evening coat carelessly thrown halfway onto an ugly armchair. Remembering all too well that he'd thrown her burgundy velveteen coat in just this careless way, Wynn valiantly tried to repress her curiosity at the circumstances of this throw. With an unladylike grunt, she thought instead, *What an odd sport for a grown man, tossing women's evening coats at chairs! He ought to take up basketball to improve his aim!* But her attempt at humor couldn't mask what she felt at this proof of some woman's presence here—was it Diane?—or her annoyance that she felt anything at all. With an exasperated sigh she snatched up the satin coat and marched back toward the foyer. At least it would give her a place to begin making order out of chaos.

She opened the door she thought must be the coat closet, and closet it was, but as big as Wynn's bedroom at home. The floor was travertine marble, like the foyer, and the walls that weren't covered either with louvered doors or mirrors were papered in an elegant abstract design in brown and gray foil. The short wall to her left and the one long unbroken wall she faced were covered with closed storage space and closets. Behind the dusty louvered doors hung several men's outer garments: a tweed overcoat, a Burberry raincoat, two suede jackets, and a down vest. A brown marble counter ran the length of the short end wall, the mirror above it lit with theatrical dressing-room lights. The counter held emergency supplies for primping: cotton puffs in a heavy cut glass bowl, facial tissues in tortoise-shell boxes, and a supply of face powder in a Japanese brown-lacquered container.

Wynn took a wooden hanger from behind the louvered doors and hung up the evening coat. Aaron Stone couldn't possibly have had anything to do with the decorating of this room, Wynn thought meanly. It was much too taste-fully done. Shrugging abruptly, she turned to leave. Still, as attractive as the room was, all it needed was a bowl for tips with a few coins at the bottom for bait. But if the man wanted to have a front hall closet that looked like a public restroom, why, more power to him. During the morning hours Wynn concentrated on doing what she could with the rooms of the penthouse. In the living room she moved what furniture she could budge into some semblance of conversational groupings, but there were several hulking couches that weighed as much as grand pianos and these she had to leave stranded where they were. Like the front hall closet, the half-bath meant for guest use was an attrac-tive room of tiled walls, marble floor, and gold-plated fixtures. But the colorless linens hanging limply on the towel bars and stacked in the cabinets beneath the counter were obviously the victims of years of harsh commercial laundering.

The kitchen too was a chef's delight, fit for a fine restaurant in layout and quality of equipment. But as Wynn investigated the contents of the refrigerator and the cupboards, she saw that Old Mother Hubbard had nothing on Aaron Stone. Even such basics as butter, sugar, and salt were in skimpy supply. In the back corner of a nearly empty cabinet, she found a jar of powdered coffee, caked with age and made herself a cup to sip as she sat at the glass and wrought iron kitchen table, making out a list of additional supplies for tomorrow's dinner.

By no stretch of the imagination was Wynn a gourmet cook, but since working at Helpmates she'd learned how to fake it quite well. One infallible trick was to use caviar in some fashion during the dinner. Since Aaron was clearly a meat and potatoes man, Wynn planned to combine the caviar with new potatoes in a recipe she'd copied from a dish served at Fournou's Ovens, a first-class restaurant housed in San Francisco's aristocratic Stanford Court Hotel. New potatoes were baked until tender on a bed of rock salt to draw out their moisture, then cut in half and the pulp scooped out and mashed. The skins were deep fried until crisp and brown, then restuffed with the potato pulp and topped with a dollop of sour cream and a generous spoonful of "golden caviar," the roe of whitefish. Wynn hadn't expected anyone's kitchen to have a supply of rock salt or even sour cream—but she hadn't thought she'd need to order vegetable oil for deep-frying!

And so it went through the rest of her planned menu. For the appetizer of crab-stuffed avocado she added curry powder and mayonnaise to her list. The lemon sherbet to serve between the heavy appetizer and the entree—another of her gourmet tricks—was already ordered, as were the salad ingredients of butter lettuce, raw mushrooms, and mandarin orange slices. But olive oil from Lucca had to be ordered for the dressing. Dessert would be several soft cheeses and, for character, a wedge of pungent Stilton, fruit in season, and French chocolate creams. The last item on her new list was a pound of freshly ground French-roast coffee beans. Imagine a kitchen without coffee of any kind! The man was barely human.

By three o'clock that afternoon all deliveries had been made, the groceries put away, and the numerous bouquets of flowers distributed where they'd do the most good. Wynn took one last tour through the rooms and, with a defeated sigh, decided she'd done all that was humanly possible to cheer the place up a bit, considering what she had to work with. The one thing left that might've been done that day was to set the table. Wynn took inventory of the table linens in the drawers of the huge sideboy in the dining room. The beautiful lace cloth she'd seen last week was there, but for the impression Wynn hoped to make, for Lula's sake, she thought the serene and venerable old standby lacked impact. However, anxious to escape before Bluebeard returned to his dungeon, Wynn decided to give the table decoration more thought during this evening at home and set it tomorrow while she cooked.

Later that evening, as she sat curled up on her comfortable sofa, warmed by a cheerful fire, soothed by Bach on the stereo, Wynn reveled in the contrast between her own cozy, attractive little house and the bleak barn where she'd spent the day. Now that she was removed from its depressing atmosphere, the significance of Aaron's chilly, barren environment began to nag at her sympathies. What could it mean that a man of his wealth lived so dismally? It was more than simple disinterest or a lack of time due to the press of business. If it were only that, wouldn't someone with Aaron's resources turn the task over to a decorator? No, there was something in it that indicated strong negative emotion, something willful and perverse.

When the doorbell rang, Wynn thought it must be Lula.

In order to keep her assignment a secret, and in order to substitute Lula's granddaughter, Meg, as Ed's father's helper this weekend, Wynn had told her boss she wasn't feeling well, and it was like Lula to make a cheering visit to an ailing friend. Therefore Wynn gave no thought to her attire—a comfortable pink velour robe and scuffs to match—as she went to the door.

When she saw Aaron there in the doorway, she gasped and clutched at the wide lapels of her robe, as if the gesture would somehow change her appearance. At the amusement on his face, her temper flared, and, taking refuge in attack, she demanded, "What are *you* doing here?"

"I want to come in and speak to you for a minute," he said mildly.

"Well, you can't come in. I'm tired. And I'm not dressed," Wynn snapped.

"You are too dressed," he countered. "You're certainly not naked. I'm sure I'd notice if you were."

Embarrassed because he was looking at her as if she was indeed naked, Wynn muttered, "Well, then, I'm not dressed for company."

Bestowing a wondering gaze on her, Aaron said dryly, "Whatever else I may think of you, I didn't think you were so vain and silly that you wouldn't speak to someone because you're not dressed to the teeth."

Wynn's eyes widened in outrage. "Considering what you've accused me of so far, I should think it was obvious that I don't want to speak to you—of all people—half undressed!"

To Wynn's surprise, Aaron looked away, receiving her remark in silence. He stood there on her doorstep looking ill at ease, and at the sight of the sober shadow that had fallen over his handsome face, Wynn helplessly felt herself soften toward him. What on earth was it about this man that made her will turn to jelly and her reason dissolve!

With an exasperated sigh, she said, "All right, come in, then, but just for a minute."

As soon as the words were out of her mouth, she saw by the satisfied smile on his full, firm mouth, that once again she'd been manipulated by a master. He closed the door behind him and stepped into the foyer. Seeing him there, where he'd stood the night she'd met him, made Wynn extremely nervous. Determined that there'd be no encore of that incident, she took a hasty step backward.

"Well?" she said briskly. "What did you want to speak to me about?"

Because Aaron hesitated so long before he spoke, Wynn had the oddest feeling that his words were substitutes for those he'd originally intended to speak. "I thought you might like to know the identity of tomorrow night's guests," he said lamely.

"If you'd like to tell me"—Wynn shrugged vaguely—"although the cook needn't know who eats her food unless, of course, someone is violently allergic to something."

Aaron frowned. "But you're not just a cook, you're a surrogate wife, of sorts. A wife would certainly want to know the identity of her guests!"

"Now, just a minute, Mr. Stone," Wynn said, alarmed. "Let's have no misunderstanding here. I am not a surrogate wife. At Helpmates we perform the *functions* a wife might perform but in no way, shape, or form do we function *as* a wife. I grant you, the distinction is subtle. But a man of your intelligence should have no trouble grasping it!"

Ignoring her correction entirely, he continued. "My sister Anne and my brother-in-law Max will be there. You'll remember them from the evening you masqueraded *as a wife*," he said with pugnacious emphasis. "Diane Donovan will also be among those present—you'll remember her from the same evening, no doubt. There will be another business associate of mine, and, of course, myself." Then, with an evil smile, he added, "So you see, except for the addition of one stranger, and the absence of good old Buckie, it'll be like old times."

Ignoring his juvenile sarcasm, Wynn commented, "That's five. An awkward number for dinner. Isn't there one more person you'd care to bestow your largesse upon?" she asked sweetly.

"Can't you even count? There are six," he said impatiently. "You make six."

Wynn felt a stab of apprehension. Coming from Aaron, this new development had to be a trap of some kind. Her mind scrambled to recall if acting as hostess had been part of the original bargain, but all she remembered him saying was that she was to prepare a dinner party which she'd taken to mean put on, in the sense of readying the house, cooking, and, probably, serving the dinner.

So now had he decided to pass judgment on her table manners too? Discover if she talked with her mouth full? Or leaned her elbows on the table? Well, she'd die before she'd let him make a fool of her again by losing her temper. She'd show Aaron Stone that Wynn Harris could take whatever he dished out—and then some!

Smiling coolly, she said, "My, my, what a democratic employer! The cook sits at table. Will wonders never cease?"

"It makes no difference to me what you call yourself," he said gruffly, "so long as I get my money's worth—just like Buckie."

Wynn's hands involuntarily clenched into fists and her shoulders straightened for combat. But before she could open her mouth to protest, Aaron glided forward and lifted a long glossy tress of Wynn's black hair in his hand.

"Wear your hair up, the way you did at lunch that day," he said in an intimate tone that sent shivers down Wynn's spine. His strong fingers insinuated themselves into the

87

soft mass of her hair, the touch of his fingertips making her sensitive scalp tingle. Cupping her head firmly in his hand, he brought her face closer and closer to his, and even as she felt herself drawn nearer to those sensual lips, she was helpless to resist. This time the kiss that covered her mouth was softly tentative, sweetly searching, and by its very hesitance coaxed Wynn's eager compliance as no amount of force could ever have done. Against her open, trembling lips Aaron whispered, "Already you've made a world of difference, little Helpmate. Perhaps there's hope for Chez Stone, after all."

Then, Aaron stepped away from her and walked to the door. With an abruptness that bewildered her, Wynn saw him abandon the role of the gentle prince and revert to the robber baron he was. "My car will pick you up at nine in the morning," he said flatly. "Please don't keep the driver waiting. I have a busy day and I'll need him myself."

Wynn stood staring at the closed front door feeling a confusion of emotions—none of them pleasant. She was resentful that this man presumed to toy with her when he pleased or insult her when that suited him. But most of all, she was angry at her own spinelessness. With a blush of shame, Wynn admitted that all it had taken was one meaningless kiss and a casual compliment about her day's work and she'd been ready to give him her all! And for Wynn Harris, of all people, daughter of a faithless Irish rake, to be taken in like that—really, it was too disgusting!

By nine fifteen the next morning Wynn was delivered to the entrance of the Standard Building, and as she got out of the sleek black limo, dressed in her jeans and sweat shirt, carrying a small valise, she saw Paul, Helpmates's resident Marxist, loping down the block toward her.

"Yo, pretty one!" he called. "I heard you were sick!"

Cursing her luck, Wynn had no choice but to wait as he came up to her, saying, "What's with the suitcase? Are you running away from home?"

Muttering that he should keep his voice down, Wynn hustled Paul into the building, then, deciding that the only way to buy his silence was to tell him the truth, she took him upstairs to the penthouse with her, filling him in on the way. "So you see, you mustn't breathe a word of this to Lula. She'd have a fit. Do you promise?" Wynn finished her recital with an anxious frown.

Paul stood in the marble-floored foyer looking about him in disapproval. "Comes the revolution," he said ominously, "there'll be no more of this disgusting conspicuous consumption by the few to the detriment of the many. If Lula would listen to me, if she'd turn the business into a co-op, she wouldn't have to traffic with the oppressors like this Stone guy."

"Be that as it may," Wynn said patiently, "do you promise not to tell her what I'm doing? She does have her pride, you know."

Paul's lean, sharp-featured face softened with a smile as he looked down at Wynn, standing so tensely before him. "That's quite a sweat shirt you're wearing, dear girl." He recited the message on the front of Wynn's shirt, "BEHIND EVERY GREAT WOMAN," then turned her around and read the back, "THERE'S A MAN WHO TRIED TO STOP HER. For someone as politically savvy as you, I'll gladly violate my principles. And I'll even help you in your devious scheme, if you want."

Wynn laughed and threw her arms around his skinny shoulders. "I knew I could count on you, Paul. And as a matter of fact, there is something you could do. I need dozens of candles, all sizes, all pastels. Would you run over to Macy's, put them on Lula's account, and bring them back up here to me?"

"As soon as I've checked in at the office for my assignments," he promised.

"Oh, and, Paul, not that I wouldn't trust you with my very life," Wynn said with a teasing grin, "but I think you should know that if Lula gets wind of this, I'll know where she heard it. And if that happens, I'll be forced to tell everyone at work that you own a goodly chunk of AT&T stock."

The smile slid from Paul's face. "You'd actually do that to me? After I confided in you during a weak moment?"

"Only if I must," Wynn said primly.

By noon everything was done that could be done. From her valise Wynn had taken one of her own fine percale bed sheets to layer under the old lace tablecloth. Its soft rosy-pink hue glowed through the lace with a charming ingenuousness, Wynn thought. Rather than a centerpiece, she planned to put a fresh pink rose and green fern from her own garden at each place setting.

The salad greens were washed and chilling in the refrigerator, ready to be put together with the other ingredients and dressed at the last minute. The avocado appetizers were prepared. The noble prime rib stood on the kitchen counter coming to room temperature and the carefully sized new potatoes were even now baking in the oven.

On the formidable sideboy in the dining room dozens of candle holders—some authentic and some contrived just for tonight—stood waiting for Paul's arrival with the candles. Nothing made a room look more festive and opulent than a blaze of candlelight, Wynn thought.

When she heard the buzzer at the penthouse door, she pushed the intercom button, and, hearing Paul's voice, pressed the release to allow the elevator to ascend to the top floor. He came in with a sulky look on his thin face, still irked that she'd threatened to expose his one venture into capitalism, and after he'd been such a good comrade too.

Thanking him profusely for running this errand for her, she took him into the dining room and asked his advice about which candles should go into which holders. When this job was done to both their satisfactions, Paul's mood had lightened.

"Are there any scraps in the palace kitchen you might throw to a hungry peasant?" he asked with mock humility.

"You won't believe this unless you see it," Wynn said, taking him into the kitchen and throwing open the cupboard doors to expose their pitiful emptiness. "All that's here is what I ordered for dinner tonight. I can make you a cup of good coffee, though."

Settling for that, Paul made himself comfortable at the kitchen table, and minutes later the two of them were enjoying the aromatic French coffee, talking shop, and laughing. Then, to Wynn's horror, she heard the front door open and close and in seconds saw Aaron Stone stalking through the dining room toward her, a black cloud on his face.

Jumping up with a hammering heart, and hating herself both for her fear of him and her servility, she hastened to introduce Paul. "This is my colleague, Paul Bennett. Paul, this is my client, Mr. Stone." The two men exchanged short nods and Wynn rushed on. "Paul was good enough to run an errand for me and we were just having a cup of coffee before he left."

As Paul, taking the none too subtle hint, rose to leave, Aaron said dubiously, "Your colleague? In what pursuit, if I may ask?"

"Why, in Helpmates, of course," Wynn said. "Paul is one of the wives."

Aaron made no attempt to hide his contempt. "Well, I suppose it stands to reason. This is San Francisco, after all, where anything goes."

Paul's lean face blanched. He drew himself up to full dignity and in a cool voice replied, "If I correctly infer what you're implying, Mr. Stone, and if what you imply were true, it would be irrelevant to my choice of work, wouldn't it? And if you think otherwise, then you're not only an oppressive capitalist and a benighted reactionary, but a social Neanderthal as well."

Wynn stood frozen with dread throughout Paul's foolhardy but courageous speech. Only when she saw the wintry smile on Aaron's mouth, did she dare to breathe again. "It's been years, I believe, since I heard anyone correctly use the words *infer* and *imply*, Mr. Bennett. Are you a writer, by any chance?"

"Yes, as a matter of fact, I am!" Paul replied in a tone somewhere between defiance and pride.

"I thought so," Aaron said with a smile of mild approval. "I often have need of writers in my business. Competent writers are very scarce, as you probably know. Perhaps we can work together sometime." And then in a sly tone, he added, "Unless you'd feel co-opted by the enemy."

Paul blushed, and Wynn was astounded to see her usually ferocious friend brought to such a state. She stood rooted to the floor as Aaron smoothly ushered Paul out of the kitchen and toward the front door, saying soothingly, "And by the way, Mr. Bennett, I was not at all implying what you inferred. I was referring to this bizarre company you work for, in particular, not the modern sexual mores of our society in general. As to that, it's true that I'm a traditionalist. But I also believe in live and let live."

The man who reentered the kitchen, however, was not the affable man who'd just left it, Wynn soon discovered. Aaron stook a stance in the middle of the room, his hands on his hips, and remarked, "Do you realize that never once have I seen you without the company of a man?"

Wynn closed her eyes in weary patience. "You've only seen me four times in your life. And two of those times, the man with me was you."

"And what was this vital errand your colleague had to run for you?"

"It was for your damned party tonight. He brought me the candles," Wynn said, throwing all caution to the winds. "And stop cross-examining me! I'm not your serf!"

"Not that your present attire isn't fetching," he said sarcastically, "but I hope you brought something suitable to wear this evening. Or did you plan to go home to change?"

"No," Wynn said, "I have a change of clothes in one of the servant's rooms."

"Oh, for God's sake!" Aaron expostulated, turning on his heel to leave the room. "You're really incorrigible, do you know that?"

In seconds he was back. "What's that mess of junk on the sideboy?"

With a killing glare, Wynn replied, "That, Mr. Stone, is my feeble effort to put some life and light into that mausoleum you call a dining room!"

Aaron snorted dubiously and sat himself down in the chair Paul had recently vacated. "I've come home for a bit of lunch. Is there anything around? Eggs? Are you good at omelets?" He watched her with closer attention than his question warranted.

Wynn's patience was sorely tried. How could one man vacillate between being an oaf and a diplomat and back to an oaf in the space of ten minutes? And what about herself, for that matter? How could she, a heretofore stable person, react to this man's moods with all the backbone of a yo-yo?

"First of all, there are no eggs. There is nothing in this kitchen except what I ordered for tonight's dinner. And second, even if there were, I was not hired as a short-order cook. If you want lunch, you'd better go elsewhere."

His voice was offensively suggestive as he said, "So you do nothing you're not hired and paid for, is that it?"

"No, that is *not* it. This entire ridiculous charade I'm going through is really something I'm doing for Lula, for nothing, because I love her and she deserves my help."

"And that kiss you gave what's-his-name in public? Was that too because you love him and he deserved it?"

Wynn's temper hit boiling point and she turned on Aaron with a fierce gleam in her eye. "There's not room in this airplane hangar you call a home for the two of us, Mr. Stone. Either you leave this very instant, or I do. And if *I* do, you can take your dinner party and all that food and—"

In another of those bewildering mood changes, Aaron hastily rose from his chair with a wicked grin on his handsome face. "I'm going! See, I'm almost gone," he said teasingly. And as he passed Wynn on his way out the kitchen door, he swooped down and brushed her lips with his.

"I know that wasn't for free, little Helpmate, but I'm more than willing to pay you for it later."

CHAPTER EIGHT

During the pre-dinner cocktail hour Wynn had her first chance in two days to relax. She sat beside Aaron's sister Anne on a lumpy settee upholstered in mold gray and watched Aaron, resplendent in a burgundy velvet dinner jacket, black trousers, and a white dress shirt, serve drinks to his guests. He was more relaxed than usual, a small, comfortable smile playing about his firm mouth. Since Wynn had nothing else to judge by, she took this to mean he was pleased with her work so far.

Unlike her brother, Anne was vocal in her praise of the temporary facelift Wynn had given the living room, and even Diane, in her less than enthusiastic manner, looked about her with eyebrows raised in surprise.

Wynn had brought from home a tried and true dress that she felt comfortable in so that she could concentrate all her thoughts on the dinner itself. In a modernized Grecian design, the neckline dropped a low V, the bodice held close to the body by cording criss-crossed between her breasts and around the waist to tie in the front. The pale blue color, the long sleeves, and the graceful fall of the skirt all combined in a serene, classical look that complimented Wynn's deep brown eyes and glossy black hair, worn upswept as Aaron had requested. The one person in the gathering unknown to Wynn was Dixon Stafford, a dignified but friendly man in his forties. Aaron introduced him to Wynn as a friend and business associate. Indeed, during this hour before dinner, Wynn gathered they were all business partners in various ventures.

When Aaron introduced Helpmates into the conversation, both as an existing business and as a new business concept, the idea was received with demeaning humor by Diane. "If that fiasco with Buckie Packard was an example of your services, Wynn, I think you'd better take the idea back to the drawing board," she said with her cool, dismissive smile.

Anne spoke up in Wynn's defense. "Knowing Buckie as you do, Diane, I'm surprised that you'd judge the entire business on an incident that was more his fault than Wynn's."

With a silvery laugh, Diane replied, "Oh, Buckie's all right. He's just an incurable romantic, hung up on love and marriage. And, after all, she did agree to pose as his wife. Didn't you, Wynn?"

From the corner of her eye, Wynn saw the expected sardonic smirk on Aaron's face. With a sigh, she admitted, "Yes, we did take the job on those terms, and we were wrong." Then, with a rueful laugh, she added, "You may be sure the evening resulted in a policy change." That is, she thought to herself, it would result in a policy change if she ever found the right way and time to confess to Lula what had happened and how it had involved her so deeply with Aaron Stone. A few minutes later Wynn indicated to Aaron that the guests should take their places at the table, and as she left the room to bring in the first course from the kitchen, she heard Dixon Stafford say, "It's an intriguing idea. There's a real need for personal service today and I think this Ms. Dobbs has found an efficient way to deliver it. It's a great improvement on the hit-or-miss scattershot methods of the past. A cleaner here, a babysitter there, a handyman here, a job gardener there. Having all services under one umbrella business makes a lot of sense."

On the way back to the dining room with the first course, Wynn heard Diane say, "The idea of personal service is sound enough, but it's so passé to dress it in the trappings of domesticity—calling the workers wives for instance. It's so fifties, isn't it? I mean, no one gives a damn about marriage anymore."

As Wynn served the stuffed avocado to muted murmurs of appreciation, she bit her lip to stifle a reply that might easily have become an impassioned and completely inappropriate lecture in defense of the married state. She flicked a glance at Aaron and was disappointed to see no sign of disagreement on his face, so she was somewhat mollified when Max came to the defense.

"Speak for yourself, Diane," Max replied, laughing. Then with a warm smile at Anne, he added, "There are at least two people at this table who care very much about marriage."

Anne looked serenely around the table, and, smiling like a wise cat, purred, "Maybe even more than two."

When everyone was served, Wynn saw that the only empty seat was at the foot of the table, opposite Aaron. She'd assumed that Diane would act as Aaron's hostess for the evening and that she herself would be paired with Dixon Stafford in the interests of gender balance at the table. But, as usual where the mercurial Aaron Stone was concerned, she was wrong.

As Wynn took her seat she glanced over at the soft glow of the dozens of candles reflected in the mirror over the sideboy. She caught her breath when she saw Aaron's reflection as well, studying her with a softness in his eyes she'd never seen before.

Anne, in her warm, friendly way, exclaimed over the table decorations, "How creative you are, Wynn, to put a colored cloth under this old lace. Mother would've approved, wouldn't she, Aaron?"

With a sardonic smile that belied his casual reply,

Aaron murmured, "Oh, yes, indeed she would. Appearances were paramount to Mother."

"And these rosebuds," Anne added quickly. "What a charming change they make from a centerpiece."

"Indeed they do," Dixon agreed, with a nod toward Wynn. "Surely this dinner speaks well for Helpmates's services, Diane."

"It's all very nice, I'm sure," Diane drawled, "but one swallow does not a summer make."

Max grinned as he ate the last bite of his shrimp-filled avocado. "You're too hard to please, Diane. One swallow of this appetizer makes it for me!"

It was just after Wynn had set the silver platter with the noble prime rib, surrounded by the caviar-topped new potatoes, in front of Aaron to be carved, that a phone call came for Anne. When she returned to the table, her usually serene expression was replaced with a look of pinched anxiety.

"Max, we'll have to leave right away. The boys both have high temperatures and Matthew has vomited twice already."

Max pushed back his chair and stood up abruptly. "I'll get our coats."

Aaron too rose from his seat. "I'm not surprised, Anne," he said worriedly. "Both boys seemed peaked at the Exploratorium this afternoon."

A random wisp of guilt flitted through Wynn's mind as she realized that after she'd been so rude to Aaron in his own home, he'd gone on to be a loving uncle to his nephews. What the two events had to do with each other wasn't clear to her, but all the same she wished now she'd fixed him a bite of lunch.

Diane's cool tone cut through the bustle at the table like a scalpel through butter. "What a shame to ruin *both* your evenings. Aaron, why don't you send Anne home in your car and Max can stay and finish his dinner at least." Then with an arch smile, she added, "Anyway, isn't it Mama who's most needed when the kiddies get sick?"

Everyone around the table, both sitting and standing, turned to stare at Diane. Aaron's brow furrowed in a formidable frown and his eyes turned cold. "I don't think you understand, Diane. You see, it's similar to an equal partnership in business." His tone lacked any trace of sarcasm, making his remark the more insulting, as if explaining a simple matter to an idiot. "Max owns fifty percent of each of these children, you see. And his halves are just as sick as Anne's."

Wynn was not surprised to see that Diane was beyond blushing. With a bored little sniff, she raised her chin and said coolly, "No need to be offensive, Aaron. I was only trying to inject a little rationality into the situation."

As Wynn and Aaron walked the worried parents to the door, Wynn offered to help in any way she could. "If you'd like me to come over tomorrow and help you nurse them, or run errands, or whatever needs doing, please let me know."

Anne smiled distractedly. "Thank you, Wynn. You're very kind, but I'm sure we'll manage. I know it's just that flu that's going around, but it is a worry."

Then, as they reached the foyer, Anne suddenly said, "Oh! Did you by any chance find my white satin evening coat somewhere in the apartment? I stopped up here last week on my way to the cleaners, then forgot it when I left."

With an absurd feeling of relief, Wynn got Anne's coat from the closet, and, repeating her offers of help, stood beside Aaron as they saw Max and Anne on their way.

Wynn felt a deep unease to see Anne go, not only because she empathized with her distress for her children, but also because Wynn saw Aaron's sister as her only ally at this strange gathering. If Aaron sensed Wynn's feelings, he said nothing, but his manner subtly changed toward Wynn during the remainder of dinner.

He was warmer and more attentive. He nodded appreciatively as he tasted each course, and his compliments were knowledgeable and detailed in a way that would have made even a real chef proud. At his most charming now, he no longer allowed Diane to dominate the conversation in her negative way, but instead steered the talk to amusing and interesting subjects, among which was photography, about which he had a remarkable knowledge.

It was during coffee and liqueurs in the living room that Diane began hiding yawns behind her fingertips. "You must get Aaron to show you his negatives or his slides or whatever," she said in her usual jaded manner. "But now, Dix, I think it's time you and I took our leave, don't you?"

The message in her tone and in Dixon's answering smile was unmistakable. Putting it together with the fact that the satin coat belonged to Anne, not Diane, Wynn suddenly understood that the relationship between Aaron and Diane was either so exotic as to be beyond her ken, or a simple business relationship. If it was the latter, she felt at once both a blissful relief and a new anxiety.

Moments later, with Aaron's firm grasp on her elbow, Wynn stood again at his side by the door, saying good night to guests. She felt a foolish little thrill, as if she were an adolescent playing house with her latest crush. And to break the spell, as soon as the door was closed she turned to Aaron and, smiling brightly, said, "Well, that's that!" and turned and made a beeline for the kitchen.

As she hurriedly scraped dishes and loaded them into the dishwasher, eager to finish and be gone, Wynn cautiously allowed herself to think that the dinner, at least, had gone well and Aaron Stone had no grounds for complaint. As she straightened up she saw with surprise that the man in question was entering the kitchen with a tray of soiled dinnerware.

"Here, let me take that—you mustn't . . . it's part of my job," she said.

"But I want to," Aaron answered smoothly. "You must be very tired; you've worked like a Trojan for two days."

Nonplused, Wynn indicated where he should set the tray and continued with her work. Aaron made several trips back and forth until he announced that the dining room and living room were now cleared. Lounging against the counter as she wiped off the stove, he said, "Should you be doing such dirty work in that lovely dress?"

Blushing at the tone of his voice that made the remark sound more like a suggestion than a compliment, Wynn replied, "It's not such dirty work if one approaches it properly."

"How do you mean?" he asked lazily. "With an apron?"

Wynn laughed. "No, I mean—well, it isn't really *dirty* work, not like cleaning out a sewer. And, of course, it depends on why one is doing it."

"Such as?" he persisted, watching her so closely that she felt the tension within her body escalate to an uncomfortable level. Glancing briefly at him, uneasy at where this line of talk might take her, she replied briefly, "Your sister, for instance. I imagine she thinks of cooking and cleaning up for her family as perhaps tedious at times, certainly repetitious but not dirty work."

"Ah, the old nobility-of-work-for-the-sake-of-love routine. But in your case . . . ?" he persisted.

"In my case it's the old nobility-of-honest-labor routine," Wynn replied tartly.

"Right you are," he said briskly, dropping the subject abruptly. "And a fine piece of work it was too." Then, with a smile so genuinely boyish and intimate that Wynn felt its impact full on her heart, Aaron added wryly, "I admit that I did my damnedest to find some fault, some flaw, no matter how small, but everything was perfect."

As he talked, Aaron enfolded Wynn within the reach of his arm and unobtrusively shepherded her from the kitchen into the living room. "And now you must sit down, relax, and have a glass of brandy with me before my driver takes you home."

So smooth was his flattery, so bedazzled was she by what she saw as a triumph for Lula, that before Wynn gathered her wits about her she found herself sitting close beside him on one of the less offensive sofas positioned in front of the fireplace. Most of the light in the vast, dim room came from the golden-red glow of the flickering embers and from a lovely jewel-toned Tiffany lamp on a large table, draped with a Spanish shawl, sitting in the corner near the fireplace.

Aaron's swarthy face seemed to attract the light from the fire and took on a burnished gleam as he spread his arms along the back of the sofa and turned his dark eyes toward Wynn with a companionable smile. Wynn looked away from those compelling eyes and took a quick nervous sip from the warmed brandy snifter.

"Wouldn't you like to kick your shoes off?" he asked. His left hand settled on Wynn's left shoulder as delicately and as briefly as a butterfly on a flower, and then, as innocuously, wafted away, leaving a trail of warmth in its wake.

Wynn sighed and laid her head back against the sofa's cushion. "I am tired," she admitted. "But I thought it went very well, and I'm glad you think so too."

Aaron shifted his body to face her more directly. "Yes, it was quite a remarkable performance."

At the use of the word *performance*, Wynn looked at Aaron quickly. There was something in his tone . . . But before she could react, Aaron added in a low, soothing tone, "You're still very tense. I can remedy that."

Wynn's lips readied themselves to produce a sarcastic smile and the reply, "I'll just bet you can," but before she could do either, Aaron's large, strong hands were warm around the base of her throat. His fingers kneaded the tight cords in the column of her neck, his thumbs pressing deep into the hollows where her shoulders met her neck. Like the breaking of a log jam, she felt the tension draining from her body, followed by a rush of sweet comfort that flowed throughout her body. Weakly she tried to push his hands away. "Thank you, but really, this isn't necessary," she said breathlessly.

Ignoring her protest, he lifted one hand to the back of her head and she felt him remove a hairpin; she felt the shift and drop of first one heavy tress of hair and then another and another until the full black mass of her hair laid in a languid tangle on her shoulders. As Wynn's eyes drooped closed, against her will, she heard Aaron release his breath in a satisfied sigh.

"I've been wanting to do that since the first night I saw you."

At these words she opened her eyes to gaze into his and saw smoldering there a look of such hot desire that she felt she *must* resist *now* while she still could. She murmured, "Aaron, please . . ."

"Aaron, please, what?" He laughed low in his throat. "Please, don't stop?"

His reply grated against the mood enough to strengthen her will to say firmly, "Please, stop!" Then, to further boost her protest, she flung his own words back at him. "Isn't this exactly what you like to accuse me of? Mixing business with pleasure?" she mocked. "Do you think you can do as you like again—and then blame me for it later?" she said with what indignation she could muster while his strong hands roamed through her hair and his wide, firm lips were but a whisper away from her mouth.

"No, no," he said urgently. "I give you my word. How can I accuse you this time? When I saw for myself that you did your job from beginning to end?" Seemingly convinced by his own words rather than Wynn's, Aaron took his hands from her face and moved away as if to give her room to think.

"This time belongs to you." Then he lowered his voice persuasively. "If you wish it, this time could belong to *us* but only if you wish it."

"I see!" Wynn cried in exasperation. "If we do things *your* way, you get what you want. And if you graciously allow *me* to choose, again, you get what you want!"

"You're telling me, then, that you want what I want?"

Wynn gasped and straightened her backbone. She'd meant only to refer to his seduction techniques which, she admitted, showed every sign of succeeding. But what she'd *said* his devious mind could easily twist into an admission that she desired him—when nothing could be further from the truth! And what gall he had to put her in the position of virtually asking him to make love to her!

"I do not want it!" she denied vehemently.

"Do you expect me to believe that?" Aaron asked softly, reaching out for her again. "Especially after that episode at your house the night we met?"

Wynn flushed and replied resentfully, "You assaulted me and you know it."

"At first, perhaps," Aaron admitted, pulling her close to him, putting his arm around her shoulders, brushing back the soft black cloud of her hair from her cheeks with his other hand. "But you responded and *you* know it. Why deny it?"

Without waiting for an answer from her, perhaps not even expecting one, Aaron gently tugged at the cording tied in a bow under Wynn's full breasts until it fell away, leaving no barrier, however small, to the zipper tab that nestled in her décolletage. A voluptuous shudder trembled through Wynn's body as she watched and heard, as in a trance, the soft whirring of the zipper moving down her body, laying bare the warm flesh beneath, covered only by beige wisps of lace.

With a sigh of submission she acknowledged the validity of Aaron's question. Why, indeed, deny that she desired him? From that first moment her eyes fell under the dark spell of his own, the night they met, she'd desired this enigmatic, mercurial, handsome man. And right now, in his overpowering presence, it was exquisitely obvious that she was fast losing control over her body's response to the magical touch of his hands and his mouth.

Wynn's fingers twined themselves in Aaron's thick, dark hair as he left a fiery trail of burning kisses scattered over her soft, willing flesh wherever his searching lips found it bare. He nipped at her sensitive ear lobe and his warm tongue tasted her skin from the long line of her neck to the hollow of her throat. Wynn gripped his shoulders in a spasm of delight as his lips lingered at the twin mounds of her breasts, his mouth gently molding first one pink nipple, then the other, already taut with desire. When the sensations grew too explosive to bear, Wynn gave a gentle tug to his wavy hair to coax his head up to meet her mouth. After a second's gleam of surprise and satisfaction in his dark eyes, he accepted her invitation with enthusiasm, covering her mouth with a sweet pressure that matched that of his body as it leaned into hers and bore her down to a reclining position on the sofa.

When Wynn felt the entire length of his taut, muscular body against her own, the heat of desire in her blood for more of him made her yearn toward him. She felt like molten gold in his hands, her flesh seeming to flow toward him wherever he touched her, wanting only to follow his lead and submit to his every wish.

But as he continued to kiss her bare skin and stroke her quivering thighs, soon it wasn't enough to lie passively back. Now Wynn was eager for the feel of him next to her bare skin, under her hands, against her lips. She searched for the buttons of his shirt, deftly undid them, and slipped her hand inside to feel the heat from his powerful chest, then moved her palm down his flat stomach and slipped her fingers into the waist of his trousers.

She felt his passion building as he moved rhythmically against her, nudging her knee aside to press his body ever closer to hers. In a voice thick and deep, Aaron whispered into Wynn's open and waiting mouth, "I want you, I want you so . . ."

Aaron's mouth grew more demanding now that Wynn had acknowledged her own pleasure, and as he kissed her with barely leashed passion, in gentle contrast his hands cupped her throbbing breasts in his palms like precious objects.

A surge of triumphant joy electrified Wynn's body at his words and she arched against him almost desperately and moaned in inarticulate surrender. At the sound, Aaron suddenly froze into stillness, like a predator sighting its victim in a green and tangled jungle. Then, with a profoundly deep sigh, he pushed himself up from Wynn's soft, warm body, leaving her chilled and bereft as if she floated alone in cold, dark space. Half-sitting, bewildered, she asked, "What is it?" then sank back onto the couch and watched as Aaron's trembling hands carefully zipped up her dress. His eyes were rueful—and something more Wynn couldn't read—as he watched every inch of beautiful, willing flesh disappear from view. Now Wynn did sit up, the better to recover her poise, since she had no idea what to say. Aaron sat beside her, his arms resting limply on his knees, staring into the fire. Finally, turning to give her a brief, baffled smile, he muttered, "I don't understand it either."

"Well, perhaps it's for the best," Wynn replied awkwardly, near tears of frustration and hurt. Did he find her unacceptable after all? Did it occur to him that the master was dallying with the maid again?

Aaron took Wynn's hand in his and, with his eyes lowered, he said, "There's too much at stake. I thought—I don't want you to think about this later and accuse me of taking advantage of you again—of presuming a situation that doesn't exist." Bewildered even further by his words, still feeling close to him, even though he'd rejected her so suddenly, Wynn tried to give him the gift of her true feelings. "I'm not sure what you're trying to say, Aaron, but you took nothing from me tonight that I didn't freely give—this time."

Aaron studied her face carefully. "But why did you give it? Why tonight?"

Wynn stood up, straightening her dress and tying the intricate cord once again beneath her breasts. More confused than she'd ever been in her life, she replied softly, "I don't know myself. Let's sleep on it, shall we?"

The wicked, intimate grin reappeared as Aaron teased, "Together?"

Wynn laughed softly and shook her head no. But her heart swelled with a tentative hope. Was it possible that beneath his stony exterior, Aaron's heart was as ready and willing to love as her own?

CHAPTER NINE

On Sunday afternoon, feeling full of self-confidence and well-being, Wynn made a friendly call to Ed Patterson to see if he was managing all right without her and to speak to the children. She was told that things couldn't be better, that the children were crazy about Meg, and at that very moment were swimming with her in the apartment's pool while Ed prepared their lunch. Naturally Wynn was happy that her absence had caused no trouble for Ed. So wasn't it odd that such cheerful news should cast Wynn into a state of brooding uncertainty?

She felt as if she'd stepped off a familiar path into the unknown. As she performed her weekend housekeeping tasks she was plagued by second thoughts about last night's events. Had she made a fool of herself again? True, the work she'd been hired to do was finished before that embarrassing lapse in decorum took place. But still, there was no denying she, the employee, had dallied with Aaron, the employer. It was only the difference between the letter of the law and the spirit of the law. In spite of Aaron's denial that he wouldn't blame her later, he *could*, with complete justification, accuse her again of the very thing that had made him distrust Helpmates in the first place: mixing business with pleasure.

She thought again and again of his words when he'd so suddenly broken away from her, leaving her weak with desire for him, wanting with all her being for him to continue.

"There's too much at stake," he'd said. "I don't want you to accuse me of taking advantage of you again—of presuming a situation that doesn't exist," he'd said.

By evening, as she sat curled up on her sofa watching *60 Minutes,* Wynn was convinced that the lovemaking between them had been a fluke of the moment, that Aaron's remarks referred to the bargain between them wherein Wynn was to prove the integrity of Helpmates, that the dinner party had earned his approval, but that her subsequent behavior had undoubtedly undone all her hard work, leaving her at square one. After all, Aaron had not given her his final decision, and surely he would have if only she'd resisted his advances and stopped while she was ahead.

To make matters even more embarrassing, she still had the key to his apartment. To keep it any longer would certainly leave her open to all kinds of unpleasant insinuations from the cynical and suspicious-minded Aaron Stone.

Therefore, instead of going directly to work Monday morning, Wynn took the elevator to Aaron's office. She gave her name to the chic young Oriental receptionist and asked her to see that Mr. Stone received the envelope in which Wynn had discreetly put the key.

"Ms. Harris, Mr. Stone left word that if you came in this morning I was to ask you to go directly up to the penthouse."

Dreading to see him again, but understanding that he, too, might have reason to want the key returned discreetly, Wynn once again made her way up to the formidable door of the penthouse and rang the bell. Some moments passed before he answered, and when he opened the door, Wynn was shocked at his appearance.

He was dressed in a long brown wool robe and slippers.

As he weakly gestured her into the foyer, she saw that his vibrant dark hair was dull and lifeless, his usually glowing eyes now had a febrile glitter, and his handsome face was gaunt and pale. As he preceded her into the living room she noticed that he was unsteady on his feet. As he began to speak he was suddenly overcome by a hacking cough and he clutched a nearby chair for support.

"Aaron!" Wynn cried in alarm, her concern for this obviously ill human being driving all else out of her head. "You must get right to bed!" And following his muttered direction and the vague wave of his hand, she led him down the hall to the bedroom she'd not yet seen. Supporting him to the rumpled king-size bed, she waited until he slowly crawled in and lay there with his eyes closed in sick fatigue.

As she looked around her at the colorless room, as devoid of personality as the rest of the apartment, Wynn wondered worriedly what to do. Clearly a man this sick should not be left alone. And Wynn recognized that, more than anything, she wanted to stay and care for him. But she was a virtual stranger to him, really. It was unthinkable that she should take such a responsibility on herself without being asked. As she watched him from the doorway, Aaron's eyes opened a slit, then closed, and with a groan he thrashed about a bit on the messy bed, then seemed to fall into a doze.

Wynn returned to the living room and reluctantly called Anne. It was a shame to add to her worries about her own sick children, but Wynn felt she had no choice but to call the only family member she knew of.

Anne answered the phone sounding frantic and harassed. When Wynn described the state her brother was in, she sighed, replying, "Well, I can't say I'm surprised, Wynn. He was here all day yesterday, right in the thick of it all, helping Max and me take care of the boys. And

110

now Max is showing signs of coming down with it too. I just hope *I* can stay on my feet."

Aware of her own unworthy and ulterior motives, Wynn said hesitantly, "Would you like me to get someone from Helpmates to stay with Aaron for a few days, Anne?"

"Oh, would you, Wynn?" Anne said, sounding greatly relieved. "I'd call his doctor if I didn't know Aaron would have a fit if I did. And I'm certain it's just this flu. Our doctor said to keep the boys quiet and warm, flood them with liquids, and wait it out. I'm sure that's all Aaron needs too. I'd be so grateful if you'd see to it for me— you'll know who's best at this kind of thing. And I'll try to get over later this evening, or tomorrow at the latest. And, Wynn, thanks so much for caring enough to call and tell me. I won't forget this."

Wynn hung up, a small, gratified smile on her lips. It wasn't that she was glad Aaron was ill, exactly. But how nice it would be to be near him, to do for him, when he was too weak to intimidate her with his wicked tongue or to confuse her with his unexpected spells of sweetness and humor, or, most of all, to seduce her with that special magic he held over her and then cast her aside, forlorn and frustrated. Now it would be she that held the power over him. It was a good feeling.

First she went back to the bedroom to look in on him. He was sleeping heavily, his hair damp, the awful limp sheets he lay on looking crumpled and uncomfortable. Then she used the telephone in the kitchen to call Sherri at Helpmates and asked to speak to Paul, since he was already an accessory after the fact.

After telling him the bare facts of the situation, she instructed him, "Go to Macy's and buy a set of the most expensive bed linens they carry and a pair of good men's pajamas and bring them up to the penthouse."

"Isn't this just a bit above and beyond the call of duty?"

Paul asked disapprovingly. "Why the most expensive linens? Because the rich have more delicate skin than us peasants?"

"I'm not asking you to buy Porthault sheets, Paul. If you could see the state of his linens, even you would agree that it's only an act of mercy to put a sick person on percale instead of worn-out, coarse muslin."

Within the hour Paul had accomplished his mission. It was only after Wynn told him how Aaron had come down with the flu that his attitude softened a bit. "Hey, that's really nice," Paul said, smiling. "I wish I'd had an uncle like that when I was a kid."

Then Wynn gave Paul the key to her house and asked him to go and pack her a small overnight bag with a nightgown, a robe, and a change of clothes. "A pair of jeans and a sweater will do. Just rummage through my bureau until you find what you need."

At the door Wynn gave him a kiss on the cheek and told him how much she appreciated his help. "I owe you a couple now, Paul. But don't forget," she said as he stepped out into the foyer, "mum's the word."

With a wry smile Paul gave her a mock salute. "AT&T's the word, more like it!"

Later that afternoon Wynn was discarding spent blossoms from Saturday night's flower arrangements and consolidating the remaining flowers into new bouquets when she heard a horrendous spate of coughing over the sound of running water from Aaron's master bedroom suite in the far reaches of the apartment.

Taking the new linens and pajamas with her, she hurried down the hall and into the bedroom to find the bathroom door open and Aaron leaning weakly against the counter while he ineptly tossed water at his feverish face with the abandon of a sea lion. He wore only pajama bottoms and they were thin with age, tied at the waist with a frazzled cord, and ragged at the leg hems. From his reflection in the mirror Wynn watched rivulets of water trickle crookedly through the crisp dark mat on his broad chest. His dark hair lay lank and sweaty against his forehead, exposing its classically sculptured shape, but adding to the general impression he made of being a shipwreck survivor.

His eyes blurred with water as she watched him grope for a towel. Without thinking she stepped forward hurriedly and supplied it from the towel bar near the lavatory. He started slightly, stared at her dully, then took the towel and mopped at his face and neck. "What are *you* doing here?" he asked in a voice raw from coughing.

"I've been here all day. Don't you remember letting me in this morning?" Wynn asked gently.

With a weak smile and a gallant attempt at levity, Aaron replied, "Surely you jest. I'd never forget such a pleasant event, and I don't remember it at all."

Alarmed at what this lapse of memory suggested about the seriousness of his illness, Wynn abandoned the tentativeness she'd been feeling about her presence here and switched easily into that state of kindly bossiness she assumed nurses must operate within.

While Aaron slumped against the bathroom counter, his usually taut, muscular stance now slack, Wynn went to the tiled shower with the opaque glass door at the end of the room and turned on the water, adjusting it to a warm, gentle flow. "A shower will do you a world of good," she said with assurance. "Just be careful not to fall over and crack your head. You're not very steady on your feet."

A sad little semblance of a leer appeared on his pale, gaunt face as he answered, "Perhaps you'd better join me, just to make sure."

Wynn smiled impersonally, instantly repressing the leap of pleasure she felt at his silly invitation. She really must keep in mind that the man was not responsible for

113

what he said or did. "There now, the water is ready. I'll leave you to it while I make up your bed. Oh, and when you're finished, put on these fresh pajamas. Both parts, please." Aaron pulled at the frazzled tie of his pants and Wynn quickly edged toward the bathroom door.

"I never wear tops—and seldom bottoms. I can't think why I have them on now," he said in a puzzled tone.

It was Wynn's surmise that, expecting her to return the key this morning, he'd bowed to convention and minimum modesty by donning the pajamas; his puzzlement now only further proved that his brain was feverish. But she replied only by saying briskly, "Never mind. While you're ill it's better to be covered up. You'll feel better for it, I promise."

Then, leaving him with another admonition to be careful in the shower, she quickly stripped the miserable sheets from his bed and replaced them with the new silky percales Paul had delivered. When the bed was made, the top sheet and light blanket turned back invitingly, and the pillows plumped, Wynn hovered uneasily at the door of the bathroom, expecting at any moment to hear an ominous thump as Aaron lost his balance and fell in the shower. Truthfully, her worry was not so much that he would injure himself fatally as how on earth she would pick him up and move him if he fell. He must outweigh her by sixty pounds at least. Worriedly peeking into the bathroom, she caught sight of his outline through the opaque shower door. Even this blurred view of his naked body took her breath away and brought a flame to her cheeks. His broad back narrowed to slim hips and the cunning shape of his tight, muscled buttocks was perfectly clear—given the generous help of Wynn's own shameless imagination.

At the first instant, when she saw him begin to turn frontward, she left him to his fate and rushed to the kitchen. There she made up a tray with the strong broth she'd concocted from simmering the leftovers from Saturday night's prime rib bones, and lightly buttered toast. She plucked one still perfect yellow rose from one of the bouquets, placed it on the tray, and returned to the bedroom.

Aaron sat looking exhausted on the edge of the bed. The cream color of the fine Egyptian cotton pajamas would have complemented the healthy duskiness of his normal complexion, but now it only added to his present pallor. He'd left the top unbuttoned, as if his strength had failed him at that point. Wynn set the tray down on the bedside table and bent to finish dressing him. As her face drew near his, and she detected the subtle aroma of his masculine scent mixed with fresh water and soap, as she felt the springy virility of the hair on his chest beneath the fine-combed material, the fingers that stumbled through their simple job trembled slightly.

When she'd finished, he looked up at her with the vulnerable, expectant look of an innocent and obedient child, and she felt her heart turn over with an emotion she'd never before felt toward a man. But this was no time to analyze it, she told herself shakily.

"Am I more socially acceptable now?" he asked with a wan smile.

"Well, you feel better, don't you?"

"Yes," he said reluctantly, "but I feel foolish too. You don't have to do all this, Wynn . . . really, I can manage on my own. I must be hideously infectious . . ."

"But you haven't dried your hair!" she said, ignoring his weak protests. She fetched a fresh towel from the bathroom, a towel that had nothing to recommend it but its dryness, and gently but firmly rubbed the dark, wavy hair. She stood facing him as he sat on the bed, and in a seemingly innocent gesture, like a tired child, he suddenly slumped forward and rested his face against Wynn's bosom and grasped her loosely around the waist. Ignoring the warm current that coursed through her body at his touch, Wynn continued her ministrations. One did not fuss at sick people; one did not chastise them for small offenses they weren't even aware they committed. With an effort to remain calm and nurselike, Wynn endured the delightful uneasiness of standing within Aaron's embrace, his face pressed against her breasts, until his lackluster hair was dry and returned to some pale imitation of its normal vigorous, gleaming state.

When Aaron was again ensconced in bed, she gave him his tray, inquiring whether the broth was now too cool to be appetizing. He took a sip, then, pretending to make a discovery, he joked, "Homemade chicken soup, I do believe!" Then, favoring her with a grateful smile, he said, "It tastes wonderful."

As Wynn sat beside him while he ate, she wondered at his docility as a patient. From what little she knew of him, she'd have expected him to be a bear. In spite of her efforts to repress the memory, she couldn't help remembering another remark he'd made Saturday night: *I want you, I want you so.* Except for that first startlement when she'd suddenly appeared at his side, he seemed actually pleased at her presence. Did she dare to hope that his remark had meant more than the physical passion of the moment?

He was nearly finished eating when she saw that his eyelids were drooping and an unhealthy flush had returned to his gaunt face. Wynn found a bottle of aspirin in the bathroom and gave him two with a glass of cool water. Then she urged him to lie down and rest. As she was leaving the room with the tray in her hands, she heard him murmur something as he turned on his side and settled into the clean, fresh bed. She only hoped it was an expression of contentment.

The rest of the evening was uneventful. Wynn fixed herself a light supper from the kitchen's meager supplies and took it into a small study she'd discovered off Aaron's bedroom. The room had no more flair or signs of house-pride than the rest of the apartment, but at least it showed signs of minimal human habitation. Wynn felt sure it was where Aaron spent most of his time when he was home. Two walls were covered with bookshelves; there was a comfortable leather sofa, a TV, and several artistic photographs were framed and hung on the walls.

From time to time during the evening Wynn looked in on Aaron, and from the once again crumpled bedclothes she saw that his sleep was still restless, but at least he was sleeping. It was nearly midnight and Wynn was mildly weeping her way through a rerun of *Now Voyager*, with Bette Davis and Paul Henreid, when suddenly she heard a sharp cry, then a strangled groan from the bedroom.

Throwing aside the quilt that covered her, she dashed into the bedroom to find Aaron struggling to rise from the bed, and when she switched on the bedside lamp she saw that his eyes were wide open and glazed with some delirious anguish. "Nooo, Mother!" he cried. "He mustn't play it—it's Papa's violin!"

"It's all right, Aaron," Wynn said soothingly, "it's only a dream, it's all right." She sat on the edge of the bed controlling his flailing arms as best she could, until eventually his agitation lessened and his distress receded to incomprehensible muttering. It wasn't until the shivering began and increased to such a point that his teeth chattered that Wynn dispensed with all convention and slipped under the covers to lie beside him to warm him. Aaron plunged toward her and burrowed into the crook of her arm, outstretched to receive him.

As she held him close to her, tucking the quilt tightly around him, smoothing the damp hair from his clammy forehead, she felt a blissful tenderness that she tried to tell herself was nothing but simple compassion. And as the moments slipped by, the shivering and mumbling gradually ceased until there was an instant of complete stillness of both sound and motion when she knew Aaron had escaped his delirium and was orienting himself in time and space.

"Wynn? Is that you?" he asked in his hoarse voice full of weak amazement.

"Yes, it's me. You had a bad dream, but it's all right now," she answered softly.

His hand lifted to touch her face, then lowered to the fleece of her robe, pushed aside the lapels, and came to rest on the soft flannel that covered her breast. "But you have nightclothes on," he said wonderingly.

"I'm staying in the study," she said quickly. "You shouldn't be alone." Then she added, "Anne knows I'm here," as if that made it more proper.

As his long body lay close against hers and beyond, she could feel his shins against her bare feet. He lay still against her, his heavy breathing the only sound in the quiet room. Then his hand delicately slipped beneath the elastic neckline of her gown and seemed to savor the warm fullness he found there. Wynn started to move away and sit up, but Aaron said urgently, "No, no, don't leave me."

"But you're fine now," she said gently.

"No, I'm not," he said, clasping her to him so she couldn't easily move. "I'm very ill." And for the first time since she'd arrived Wynn thought she detected a bit of the old manipulative Aaron in that seemingly manufactured self-pitying remark.

But how could she be sure? He was, after all, very ill. What a prig she'd be to jump to erroneous conclusions when all the man wanted was a bit of comfort after a terrible nightmare!

But in the dim light Wynn smiled in self-mockery. She was kidding no one, herself the least, to pretend that what she was feeling could be labeled "comforting a sick man."

Then Aaron made a very deft movement, for a sick man, that left Wynn enclosed within his embrace instead of her holding him. He burrowed his face into her neck

118

and whispered, "I won't kiss you." She felt his feverish lips against her throat as he murmured, "On the lips, that is." That same helpless, narcotic feeling coursed hotly through Wynn as she moaned and turned toward him and reveled in the sensation of his strong arms around her, his dark head nuzzling into the hollow of her now bare shoulder, his hard body pressing against her. And Wynn acknowledged her own response in the throbbing of the most secret, guarded places of her body.

Now Aaron's hand gently pushed up Wynn's gown to expose her even more fully than that night she'd been helpless to resist him. Tonight there wasn't even the protection of wisps of lace between his dark eyes and her total nakedness. A shudder of pleasure followed his hand as he stroked her body from breast to thigh, as he placed his palm flat against her quivering belly and moved his fingers in soft, gentle patterns, causing Wynn to shudder with longing.

"What a beauty you are," Aaron whispered huskily, gazing at her nakedness in the shadowy light, watching the rise and fall of her eager, swollen breasts. At his words Wynn succumbed to an even deeper level of desire and clasped Aaron's hard body to her heart as if she could enclose him within herself forever. The skin of his back felt like warm satin to her sensitive fingers and she breathed the aroma of him deeply into her lungs. With a smoothly sinuous motion Aaron lifted his body to lay with sweet weight on Wynn's and she accepted him with eager delight.

"You *do* want me, don't you." It was not so much a question, Wynn realized, as a plea for reassurance.

She opened her lips to tell him that she *did* want him, wholeheartedly and desperately, when Aaron was suddenly taken with a racking cough and fell back from Wynn, doubled up with the force of the attack.

She immediately came to her senses at the horrible

119

sound and the sight of his handsome face distorted with effort. As he struggled to catch his breath, Wynn pulled her gown down and sat on the edge of the bed straightening her robe.

"Damn," he gasped, when the fit had finally spent itself.

Wynn smiled sympathetically. "It's just as well, Aaron. You're really not up to that sort of thing."

She was rewarded with that rueful, boyish grin that always touched her heart. "A man is always up to that sort of thing but I will admit that it was unforgivably thoughtless of me to expose you to this terrible bug I have."

"It doesn't matter," she replied softly. "I never get sick. Do you think you can sleep now?"

He lay back against the pillows and grinned wickedly. "I could've slept a lot better if . . ."

Wynn laughed, turning her face to hide the blush she felt on her cheeks, and started to leave the room. "I'll be in the study if you need me—for *nursing*," she said with mock severity.

"Wynn?" She turned to listen and he said haltingly, "You aren't—angry, then? After you've been so good to me, I'd hate to think I'd taken advantage of your kindness."

Wynn shook her head slightly and murmured, "You're the one who's ill. Perhaps I took advantage of you."

Aaron studied her face with great intensity and a question in his still smoky eyes. Then he grinned and said, "Well, anyway, it's a fine way to get to know someone better, don't you think?"

CHAPTER TEN

Aaron slept through the night and the next morning he seemed somewhat improved. His eyes had lost that glazed, feverish look and a little color had returned to his face. Therefore, thinking he was more "infectious" when healthy than when ill, Wynn kept her distance from him and handed him his breakfast tray at arm's length.

"Was I that bad last night?" he asked, smiling, as he noticed her standing by the bed beyond his reach.

"No, you weren't bad; you had a very disturbing dream, that's all," Wynn said, thinking it best to ignore what had taken place between them, for, after all, in a way, neither of them had been quite responsible for their actions.

"Did I say anything?" Aaron asked curiously.

"Something about your father's violin; it didn't make much sense."

Aaron frowned and turned his attention to his tray. Poking the soft-boiled egg with a spoon, he remarked, "This is a perfectly cooked egg. You let it come to room temperature before you boiled it, didn't you."

Wynn hesitated, then nodded. The egg had come to room temperature before she'd cooked it, but only by accident. It didn't seem necessary to admit that there were two runny eggs resting at the bottom of the garbage disposal and another ruined attempt in her own stomach.

Wynn stayed long enough to make sure Aaron drank a full eight ounces of orange juice; then she left him to call

Anne and report his improvement. Anne said she would drop by later that morning to look in on her brother and stay for a short visit with Wynn.

When Anne arrived a few hours later, Aaron was again asleep. The two young women stood at the door to his room, whispering. "He looks fairly normal to me," Anne said softly. "Except, of course, I've never before seen him asleep at ten o'clock in the morning. That alone shows how sick he is."

"You should have seen him yesterday," Wynn replied. "He looked like death warmed over."

Wynn quietly closed his door, and they went to the kitchen where Wynn had prepared a fresh pot of coffee and cinnamon toast—all she'd been able to scrape up from the barren cupboards. Anne settled back in one of the white wrought iron chairs and smiled expectantly at Wynn.

"I'm so pleased that you took him on yourself, Wynn. Now I'll be sure he's in good hands."

Something unspoken in Anne's tone made Wynn shy away from pursuing that line of conversation. Instead, she asked about the boys and Max and learned that they'd reached the irritable stage—a good sign of impending health, but very tedious for the nurse. "You'll see," she admonished Wynn, "my brother will be biting your head off and ordering you around by tomorrow!"

Wynn laughed and admitted her surprise that Aaron had been such a docile patient so far. Anne tasted her coffee, then she added another spoonful of sugar and stirred it in with a thoughtful expression on her pretty, open face. "It doesn't surprise me, really. Aaron is a very healthy person generally, and when he does come down with a small ailment—a cold or a backache—he's very stoic about it. But when he was small he had his full share of the usual childhood illnesses, and that was about the only time either of us got much attention from our mother." Here Anne grinned ruefully. "So you can imagine that it was more pleasant than not for us to be ill. I think we both made it last as long as we could."

"And now that he's come down with something fairly serious . . . ?" Wynn questioned.

"Yes," Anne laughed, "he's reverting to childhood and in order to prolong the TLC—which I have no doubt you've provided him with—he's being a good little boy, to make it last longer!"

Wynn was touched, and a bit disturbed, at this glance into Aaron's childhood. It was a sad and alien notion to her that a child had to be sick to receive attention from his mother. Wynn's own mother had shown her love for her every day of her life. Surely such a serious lack might account for a child growing up to be a mistrustful cynic.

Anne's remark about her childhood seemed to have put her in a reminiscing mood, and as she told Wynn more about her background, Wynn was surprised at the parallels to her own. Aaron and Anne's father was also a musician, but on a much grander scale than Wynn's father. Abraham Stone was a concert violinist, famous and much in demand in Europe, more so than in his own country. There was luxury and a great deal of money but very little family life. Their father spent the majority of his time touring abroad while his wife and children lived in San Francisco. Unlike Wynn's father, however, he remained a husband and father, although a long-distance one, and continued to support his family and return to them between concert tours.

Their mother was a great beauty, a charming but weak and immature woman who turned her children over to governesses and housekeepers while she found solace and company in her loneliness from men drawn to her by her stunning beauty and her generosity with food and drink, and from women whose lives were as shallow and frivolous as her own.

Anne finished her confidences by saying with a self-mocking smile, "So you see, we were poor little rich kids."

"It's very sad when children are unhappy—rich or poor," Wynn said with sympathy. "You know, last night Aaron had a terrible nightmare and he mentioned his father's violin."

"Oh, really? Can you remember what he said?" Anne asked.

"Yes, I can remember exactly. He said, 'No, Mother, he mustn't play it! It's Papa's violin.' "

With a shadow in her round brown eyes, Anne shook her head sadly. "So he's still having that dream. I'd hoped he'd outgrown it by now. Poor Aaron. He suffered so at what he saw as Mother's disloyalty to Papa." Wynn rose from the table to pour fresh coffee. She wondered, but didn't want to ask, if Mrs. Stone had actually been unfaithful to her husband in his absence. Perhaps the question was plain on her face, for as she returned to the table, Anne went on in a musing tone.

"I really don't think she ever . . . actually . . . but there were always so many men—and women also, to be fair—at what she called her at-homes. There was one man in particular that Aaron and I both detested. Looking back now, I think he was a real gigolo—Mother was never very discriminating in her choice of friends—and this man would clown around for the amusement of the others, using one of Papa's violins in the most belittling, disrespectful ways. For instance, he'd act out the role of a strolling Hungarian gypsy, parodying folk songs in the most maudlin way possible. Or sometimes, with the help of a toady, he'd pretend the violin was an organ and he'd play the role of an organ grinder while this other fool would be the monkey and go around the room begging pennies from the other guests. Aaron hated it so. I know he saw it as a symbol of all that was wrong between our parents. And on one of these at-home parties, I remember

124

he went into hysterics and was humiliated in front of them all by being scolded and sent to his room without his supper."

Wynn's throat ached for the proud, sensitive child the man she knew now must have been. "How terrible for him—for you both," she said softly.

"It was worse for him, I think," Anne said. "I know it poisoned him against women in general and family life in particular." Anne looked directly at Wynn as she said, "It's going to take an extraordinary woman to prove to him that he's wrong, that all women aren't shallow and weak like our mother and that all marriages aren't the sham our parents' was." Then she laughed ruefully but with real distress beneath the lightness. "Even Max and I, as happy as we are, don't seem enough to convince him. He just thinks we're the exception that proves the rule."

Hesitantly Wynn asked, "Then he's never . . . been serious about a woman?"

Anne shook her head firmly. "Never. He's a hard case, Wynn."

"I thought, at first, maybe he and Diane . . ."

"Diane least of all!" Anne said, laughing shortly. "He associates with her because she's so 'unwomanly'—as he sees it. He likes her as a business associate because she's so much 'like a man.' "

Anne left soon after this, saying she hoped Wynn would forgive her boring recital of her family background. But Wynn was far from bored with what she'd heard. She was fascinated, even grateful. So much was clear now that had been either puzzling or infuriating before. How true it was that to know all was to forgive all. Wynn didn't know *all* about Aaron Stone, but she knew enough to forgive quite a lot.

By the next day Aaron felt well enough to be up for short periods of time. In the kitchen Wynn fed him lunch from the groceries she'd had delivered instead of on a tray in his bedroom. He'd dressed in a pair of beige corduroy slacks and a black turtleneck shirt that highlighted his still pale face. His dark wavy hair had not yet reached its previous sheen, but it no longer had the dusty look of black soot. She'd fixed a mushroom omelet, because an omelet was what he'd asked for last Saturday when she'd so callously refused to give him lunch, and she sat at the table with him while he ate. When he'd finished, and had expressed his compliments for the meal, Wynn tried to coax him back to bed for a nap.

"No, I'm sick of that room," he said a bit petulantly. Then, with that mercurial change of mood, he smiled slyly at her and added, "Unless you'll join me?"

Ignoring the remark, she offered a compromise. "Why don't I fix you a comfortable spot on one of the sofas in the living room. I'll sit with you, if you like, and it will give you a change of scene." He agreed to that, and soon he was propped up with pillows on a sofa with a view of the entire city, covered with a light quilt. Wynn sat nearby in a chair.

When she noticed that his gaze wandered to the busy city streets so far below, she asked, "Do you miss being out there?"

"Not really," he said, turning his attention to Wynn. "Have there been any calls from the office?"

"Your secretary called early this morning to say everything was under control. There was some problem with a Mr. Bannister's loan, but Ms. Donovan would see to it, she said."

He nodded as if the news held very little interest for him. "And speaking of business, does Helpmates get this kind of assignment very often?" he asked, gesturing toward himself.

Wynn hesitated, not knowing how to answer him. Obviously he was assuming that her sojourn here with him was an assignment—and it wasn't. She'd continued her ruse with Lula by asking for a few days off, and Lula, not the world's finest administrator at best, and at present distracted by her own worries, had agreed to Wynn's request with her customary vagueness. But Wynn didn't want Aaron to know she was here for—for what? She couldn't explain her reasons to herself, much less to Aaron.

She answered evasively, if not quite untruthfully. "No, not nearly as often as other kinds of assignments."

Aaron studied Wynn's face then moved down her body, taking in the informal plaid shirt and well-fitting, worn jeans. "I've wondered how you happened to get into this line of work," he asked curiously.

Remembering the many nasty remarks he'd made about Wynn's "line of work" in the past, she replied tartly, "I'm assuming that now you're admitting my work with Helpmates is a legitimate personal service?"

With a grin that lit up his face but showed no evidence of guilt or apology for his past meanness, Aaron nodded. "For the time being, yes," he teased.

Wynn told him a little about her background, but no details—that she'd been obliged to find work after graduation from high school and had done the usual work open to unskilled persons—clerking at Macy's, waitressing, two years as a bank teller at Wells Fargo, then finally a year as a temporary office worker.

"But what I really liked best, what I was actually good at, was domestic work. Not just the drudgery part, but the creative part too." Wynn hesitated before she added, "I had a very fine role model, you see." Now that she knew what she did about Aaron's childhood, she had no wish to rub any salt in his wounds. "My mother taught me that the occupation of housewife was a creative one—demanding, but rewarding. So when I saw Lula's advertisement for Helpmates it seemed made to order for me. And it has been."

"I don't follow your reasoning," Aaron said with a sudden reserve in his tone that bewildered Wynn. "From

127

what you've said, it's marriage that seems made to order for you, not working at Helpmates."

Embarrassed, and not even knowing why, Wynn replied a bit defensively. "Well, I suppose you're right. Helpmates is a substitution until the real thing comes along." It angered Wynn that Aaron should be able to make her feel foolish to want marriage and a family, as it were some unworthy, degrading ambition.

"And how do you feel about children?" he asked in the tone of a grand inquisitor.

Wynn's raised her chin and her voice took on a belligerent tone. "I grew up believing that there can be no more important job in the world than that of raising children. After all, a child is the basic natural resource of the world. Without properly loved and cared for children, all other resources are ultimately useless."

Carried away by her strong feelings on the subject, Wynn now continued in a lecturing tone. "Too bad the rest of society doesn't agree! Did you know, for instance, that in a government publication of job descriptions, childcare is lumped in with unskilled labor such as feeding slop to swine and sweeping up factory floors! Can you imagine? And do you realize that on the open market childcare is worth an average one dollar an hour, while the services of an interior decorator are worth an average thirty-two dollars an hour? How's that for a society whose value system is turned upside down?"

When Wynn had vented her feelings enough to once again notice Aaron, she saw that he was looking at her with a look of suspicious disbelief on his face. Now, what on earth had she said to make him look like that?

Aaron raised himself from the nest of pillows and sat upright on the sofa. In a dry, cool voice, he asked, "Have you ever received a marriage proposal, Wynn?"

Taken aback by this question that seemed to come out of left field, Wynn answered carefully, "Yes. Three."

"Three! And you refused them all?"

"Obviously," Wynn replied, alert now to the change in his manner.

"Why? Did you care nothing for any of them?"

"Yes, I cared for them," Wynn replied, "but not enough. I'm not dependent on a man to be able to do the work I enjoy, so I'm able to take my time until Mr. Right comes along," Wynn said, intending that Aaron should remember that he'd said the same thing to her himself—but insultingly—the night she'd met him.

But Aaron refused to be sidetracked, it seemed. His eyes held a determined intensity that frightened Wynn and his voice was strange and strained as he persisted in his questioning. "Were any of these suitors of yours rich?"

Now Wynn thought she detected the drift of his questions and it angered her. "No, they weren't."

Smiling coldly, he said, "Perhaps that had something to do with your refusal."

A flare of fury leaped up in Wynn, and a sick feeling of betrayal too. What an idiot she'd been to think that the unhappiness of a young boy could really excuse the insufferable arrogance of a man in his mid-thirties! And she'd let this man touch her intimately! She'd wanted to become one with him. It made her sick to think of it now.

In an icy voice Wynn answered, "I've just told you, by implication, that a man's money could have nothing to do with my refusal or acceptance. I don't need any man's support to live as I wish to. I'm doing that already, on my own. In fact," she added with relish, "I'd prefer *not* to marry a rich man," she continued recklessly, "or a worldly man, or a handsome man. I find such men in general to be demanding, unreasonable, selfish, and arrogant!"

Aaron's dark eyes narrowed to menacing slits. "But it's all right to work for a rich man?"

"Yes, of course," Wynn replied airily. "I see no need to discriminate against the rich, however I may feel about them personally. They need domestic help just as ordinary people do"—she looked pointedly around her at the dreary room—"in fact, sometimes even more so."

"It's fortunate for me that you feel as you do about the rich," Aaron said sarcastically. "You've done a very creditable job here these past few days. I've been aware of no discrimination at all. On the contrary, I've even felt from time to time that you . . . liked me a little, personally. But of course, that just proves how good you are at your work, doesn't it? No matter what the job, you give it that special warm Harris touch, don't you?"

They exchanged an unfriendly measuring look. Then Wynn asked coolly, "And you? Have you ever received a proposal of marriage?"

"Of course not!" Aaron snapped.

"How sad for you," Wynn murmured. "And at your age too. Perhaps you'll end up a spinster."

"Very funny, I'm sure," Aaron growled. "And even if I *had,* I would have refused, just as you have."

"Oh? And may I know *your* reasons?" Wynn asked sweetly.

"That's simple," Aaron said shortly. "Anything marriage can give me I can acquire elsewhere, and at less cost and infinitely less bother."

Wynn retorted, "What a ridiculous thing to say! There is much one can't buy in life, Mr. Stone."

"Aaron!" he snarled.

"Aaron, then."

"Such as?" he sneered.

"Such as love and friendship and loyalty."

"Those abstracts aren't guaranteed by marriage either," Aaron pointed out smugly.

"Well, one thing you can't have without marriage is children," Wynn persisted.

Aaron laughed unpleasantly. "How can you say that, living in America today? There are all kinds of ways to

130

have children without marriage, as misguided as most of those ways are. But since I don't want children anyway, that hardly seems like a clinching argument to marry."

All her best arguments demolished now, Wynn fell back on sarcasm. "You must be a very contented and happy man."

"I'm happy enough," he replied, glaring at her.

"Yes, all your requirements of life are so easily come by, aren't they? All you'll ever need is plenty of money, and that, you have. In fact, you epitomize Oscar Wilde's definition of a cynic: a man who knows the price of everything and the value of nothing!"

Aaron grunted and dropped his eyes. "Speaking of money, how much is this professional tender loving care I've received the past few days going to cost me?"

Wynn's heart felt as if it were crumbling within her breast, but her cool voice and her head held at a haughty angle belied her feelings. "Just like in real life," she said sardonically, "the wives are never directly involved in the payment process. You'll be billed by Helpmates when the assignment comes to an end."

"The assignment has come to an end, right here and now," Aaron said angrily. "You're free to leave at any time. You can chalk up another good job well done and return to your cozy little lair and bask in your precious single independence."

Wynn rose from her chair, her heart angry and aching. She walked swiftly to the small study and packed her few belongings in her overnight bag. When she walked to the living room where Aaron was still sitting, she made a great show of placing his key on the table in the foyer.

She let herself out, closing the door carefully and quietly behind her, and descended in the elevator, thinking how perverse life was. Until those last few moments, the last three days, spent in a sickroom, in a gloomy, dreary penthouse, were three of the happiest, most fulfilling days of her life.

What a fool she'd been to think for an instant that a man like Aaron Stone would have room in his rocky, wizened heart for the kind of love that she yearned to have in her life.

CHAPTER ELEVEN

The following morning Wynn reported to work at Helpmates and was relieved to be among her co-workers again after the alternating periods of exhilaration and despair during the last three days she'd spent in the company of Aaron Stone.

Lula looked her usual Easter-egg self, her silvery hair set off by a hot pink pantsuit with orange piping on the lapels and edges of the jacket. With a loving hand heavily laden with rings, she reached up and drew Wynn down to the seat next to her at the big round table. As the other wives drifted in, Lula said to Wynn in a low, confidential tone, "It was brilliant of you to think of asking my Meg to take over your father's helper assignment for Ed Patterson last weekend, Wynn, dearest."

"Oh, no, not at all," Wynn demurred, not wishing to be praised for a maneuver that was less than straightforward, especially considering that nothing but more disaster had come of it.

But Lula went on, smiling indulgently. "Of course, I'm sorry you were ill, but it all worked out so well. Meg loved the assignment and now she's agreed to join our staff for a trial period of six months instead of running off to God alone knows where with that feckless young man. And it's all thanks to you, Wynn."

Wynn's spirits sank as she thought of how poor Lula

would feel when she learned just how much she did indeed have Wynn to "thank" for!

When everyone had gathered at the table, Lula dealt out assignments from her three by five cards. A working couple had bought a house in the city's Richmond district and they needed someone to be on hand to let in various workmen and delivery people. Paul took that job because he currently needed an inactive task in order to finish polishing his manuscript, "The Downward Mobility of Upper Class Offspring in the Post-Vietnam War Era," which he planned to submit to the *Partisan Review*.

Marie, the eldest and most maternal wife, was given a sad assignment of indefinite length to cook dinner for a family and stay with the children during the evening while the parents went to the hospital to sit by the bedside of a dying grandparent.

Crisply Lula read from the third card. "A single woman needs a wife with basic mechanical aptitude to fix things around the house, to hang pictures, unjam the garbage disposal, put up bookshelves, install a rheostat on the dining room light fixture, and so forth."

Wynn raised her hand. "I'll take that." Over the years she and her mother, between them, had learned to do and fix nearly everything of a simple nature around the house.

But Lula said, "No, this woman is a sexist. She insists that only a man will fill her needs." With a little smile around the table, Lula handed the card to Jack.

With a grin and a flush that spread into his curly blond hair, Jack took the card with a mock flourish. The others responded with bawdy laughter and knowing remarks. Marie crowed, "Better not let your lady doctor hear about this one, Jack!" And Paul, in his sardonic way, commented, "If the lady has any needs that you can't meet, Jack, I'll be glad to help you out."

Fresh from her battles with Aaron Stone, Wynn was struck by the fact that even the wives themselves, who were so often the target of this very kind of sexual teasing from clients, indulged in it so spontaneously themselves whenever the situation invited it. How fraught with anxiety the whole male-female relationship is, Wynn thought in wonder.

The next job came from a man who wanted a wife to meet an old war buddy of his at the airport and take him around to see the sights of San Francisco until the client finished his work day. Again Wynn volunteered for what she saw as a pleasant, relaxing few hours of sight-seeing—something she, as a native, seldom got a chance to do. But again Lula thwarted her and gave the job to Mavis, who used to be a cab driver, and knew the city better than anyone, and was used to dealing with tourists.

Everyone had an assignment now except Wynn and young Meg, who sat quietly across the table from her grandmother, filing her already perfect fingernails. "This last assignment comes from a friend of mine who needs help for her granddaughter and is physically unable to deal with the situation herself. The granddaughter has two toddlers under three years old, and is bringing a newborn home from the hospital tomorrow. Her twenty-two-year-old husband has flown the coop."

A general murmur of sympathy followed Lula's job description, and Wynn, empathizing with the poor girl, thinking of her own mother's abandonment, again volunteered. But Lula threw Wynn a warning glance and replied smoothly, "Since this girl is so very young, I think she might feel more comfortable with someone very close to her in age. I believe we'll let our new wife have this assignment."

Understanding that Lula was probably right, and also that she wished her own granddaughter to see the poor girl as an object lesson, Wynn made no further comment. Instead, since this lack of assignment gave her a free weekend, Wynn determined to invite Ed to dinner Saturday or

Sunday evening. It was time she picked up her own life again, after it'd been so rudely interrupted by Aaron Stone.

Before dismissing her work force of wives, Lula announced that she had an important announcement to make. "Some good news and some bad news. A. J. Stone's sometime business partner, Diane Donovan, has notified me that the two of them are willing to help us out."

Wynn didn't believe it. After that last bitter scene, he'd never lend Lula money, she thought. Diane must be going on a decision they'd made perhaps Sunday—after the dinner party—but before that last fiasco between himself and Wynn on Wednesday.

"We have our Wynn to thank for this," Lula continued, smiling indulgently at Wynn. "Ms. Donovan told me that A. J. Stone asked Wynn to plan and serve a dinner party as an example of Helpmates's work, and the job she did impressed him very much." Lula reached over to pat Wynn's hand. "This was all done without my knowledge, outside our regular channels, and I consider it an act of loyalty above and beyond the call of duty."

The others all expressed their relief and congratulations that Wynn had saved Helpmates from its downfall. But Wynn inwardly cringed at being praised for what she knew could be only a short reprieve. When the events caught up with themselves, Lula and the wives wouldn't be so grateful for what Wynn had done for them!

"Now," Lula continued, "for the bad news. They will only help us out in return for an equity position in the company."

"How much equity?" Paul asked suspiciously.

Lula sighed, her smile now replaced by the worried frown they'd all grown accustomed to seeing on her once cheerful face. "Fifty-one percent," she replied.

Groans of dismay and disappointment greeted this

news, for all the wives were well aware that sole ownership of the company was very important to Lula.

"Is that our only alternative?" Jack asked. "Couldn't we get the loan somewhere else?"

"God knows I've tried, Jack," Lula replied wearily. "The usual institutional lenders won't even consider it because of our shaky financial position and lack of collateral. And the interest rates demanded by the secondary lenders are sky high. We could never meet the debt payments. I'm afraid it's this offer, or nothing."

Paul said doggedly, "You know, Lula, communal ownership of small businesses is the coming thing in this country and high time! I know all sorts of people who are involved in cooperatives of one kind or another. We could all buy into Helpmates and run it by committee—"

"Oh, lay off, Paul!" Jack shouted. "You know Lula doesn't want any part of that! If you're so keen on it, why don't you start your own damn communal business!"

"Now, now, Jack, Paul means well," Lula said in the tone of a beleaguered mother. "Let's let it rest for now. They don't require an answer until the end of this month. Maybe something will turn up by then."

As the wives drifted disconsolately out of the office, Lula asked Wynn to wait while she finished up a few details in her private office so they could lunch together. Wynn perched on the corner of Sherri's desk, staring out the window, seeing the approximate view she'd seen from Aaron's penthouse earlier in the week but from much lower down. From here people on the street looked real, not like specks in a god's eye.

How unfair it was that one man had such terrible power over others. Wynn knew she'd have to confess all to Lula soon. She couldn't go on letting her think she had even as much as the unsatisfactory offer of help she thought she had.

"By the way, Wynn," Sherri said, breaking into her

concentration, "I've had two phone calls from Mr. Stone today wanting his bill for three days' nursing care, and I have no record of any such work order. Do you know anything about it?"

"Just ignore him," Wynn said shortly.

Aghast, Sherri repeated, "Ignore him? Ignore A. J. Stone?"

"Yes! He's not a *god,* you know," Wynn retorted with misplaced sharpness.

During lunch at a wonderful French café around the corner, Lula confided her worries to Wynn about Aaron's offer. "They'll constantly want to interfere, they'll want to make a lot of changes, I just know it. And with fifty-one percent ownership, who can stop them? It won't really be my business anymore," she said sadly. "You know, Wynn, all my life I've worked for someone else. And as happy as I was with my Harry, God rest his soul, I count those years of marriage as working for someone else. If I have to go back to that, at my age, I'd just as soon retire and do volunteer work. At least I'd be free of the hassles of running my own business."

"And Wynn, I haven't even told you the worst yet," Lula continued. "After Diane Donovan called, *he* called too."

Wynn stared at Lula. Perhaps she wouldn't have to confess now. No doubt Aaron had told Lula the whole awful story in his own inimitable way.

Lula went on. "He confirmed their offer, but he also wants you to come and act as his full-time temporary housekeeper until we find him an acceptable permanent housekeeper."

Wynn gasped in surprise. "He wants me to come and work for him? Did he say anything else?"

Lula shook her head. "No, nothing else. And he only wants you until we find him a permanent housekeeper."

"An *acceptable* housekeeper, you said," Wynn pointed

out. "Hell could freeze over before that happens. You don't know him the way I do," she said, then abandoned that line for fear it would lead to more confessions than were necessary now. Wynn saw his plan clearly. He was using that last argument between them when, admittedly, she'd thoroughly insulted him, to blackmail her into returning to the penthouse for some twisted, sinister reason of his own. Unless she wanted the whole truth to come out and discredit her with Lula, Wynn knew she'd have to do as he wished.

Lula's manner was depressed as she said, "He sure doesn't mind throwing his weight around, does he? Now he's treating us as if we're an employment agency. If we didn't need his help so much, I'd tell him to go find his own housekeeper!" Then, with a sudden surge of indignation, she said firmly, "Even so, I don't think you should do it, Wynn."

"Let's not be hasty, Lula," Wynn said quickly. She needed time to think through this new development, but in the meantime her main concern was still to save Helpmates, and as long as Aaron still had the upper hand, it wouldn't do to alienate him any further. "We're so close to success now, Lula, maybe if we just hang in there we can get him to improve his terms."

Lula sighed and shrugged. "Maybe you're right, Wynn. I think it's too much to ask of you, but . . . The two of them are known around the city as hard bargainers, and now I'm seeing it first hand. You see what he's really doing, don't you? By tying up the full-time services of one of my most valuable employees, he's essentially weakening Helpmates even further. Even though he'll pay you well and we'll get the usual commission, he's still taking you out of circulation so you can't generate any referral business."

The two women sat silently, each brooding on her own particular problems caused by this formidable man. Lula sighed again. "To make matters even worse, our rent will double beginning October first when the new lease begins."

"Double!" Wynn cried furiously. "It's already exorbitant." Then, with a mean, gloating laugh, she muttered, "For once, *he'll* suffer too."

"What do you mean?" Lula asked.

"The only way someone like him *can* suffer—in his pocketbook. Imagine the rents he pays now on that enormous office and that ratty penthouse. His rents will double too."

Lula responded with a hollow laugh. "He's our landlord, honey. He owns the building."

In a small, defeated voice, Wynn replied, "Oh, I see. Well, I might've known."

CHAPTER TWELVE

By mid-afternoon on Friday, Wynn realized that she'd caught the flu from Aaron. Feeling as if her bones had been through a scrap-metal crusher, she called Lula at the office. "Lula, if it's possible for a dog to be as sick as I am then I'm as sick as a dog. Can you get someone to take Professor Jenkins for me tonight? We were going to start reading *David Copperfield*. Between you and me, I think his eyes are healed now, but he likes the company. Be sure you send someone congenial."

Lula assured Wynn she would take care of it, then Wynn added weakly, "And, Lula, I'm going to take that housekeeper job."

"No, Wynn, honey, I don't want you to. Enough is enough already."

"Yes, Lula, we have to. If I don't, it would be just like him to withdraw his offer. Let's keep our options open for a while, at least until you decide what to do about his terms." After pausing to cough, Wynn joked, "I'll try to find him a permanent housekeeper in a hurry. I'll put an ad in the *Chronicle:* Masochist wanted for slavery in a dingy penthouse."

Later that evening Wynn was awakened from a feverish doze by the phone. The sound of Aaron's deep voice directly in her ear sent shivers through her, as sick as she was.

"Hello there!" he said cheerfully, as if nothing unpleasant had ever taken place between them. "Have you heard the good news?"

"No," Wynn replied coolly. "I haven't heard any good news since last Wednesday when you released me from your august presence."

After a short silence he asked in a long-suffering tone, "Okay, Wynn, what's your problem now?"

"I'm not the one with the problem."

"Didn't Lula tell you about my proposition?"

"Yes, she did," Wynn admitted. "Now, what's this good news you spoke of?"

She heard a gusty sigh in her ear and she could picture Aaron's dark eyes narrowing with impatience. "All right, Wynn. You may not like the terms, but they're perfectly ethical, even ordinary terms under the circumstances. Besides, it's none of your business anyway."

"No," Wynn replied coldly, "and if you have your way, it's going to be none of Lula's business either!"

"That's your bias against the well-to-do speaking," Aaron said with maddening loftiness. "But be that as it may, until Lula decides what she wants to do, I assume Helpmates will regard me like any other client and send me the housekeeper I requested."

"But why me!" Wynn demanded. "Haven't you persecuted me enough?"

In a silky, soothing tone, Aaron replied, "I want you because you're the best she has. You're capable and efficient and resourceful." In spite of her anger Wynn felt herself softening to his compliments, when he added sarcastically, "But mostly because you're so democratic and tolerant about working for the rich. I'll expect you Monday morning at eight sharp," he said, reverting to a businesslike voice. "Please don't be late. I have an appointment in Sausalito at nine and I'll want to give you your instructions before I leave."

"Yes, master," Wynn muttered.

"Oh, and one other thing. Please see to it that I receive my bill for your nursing services. I don't like debts hanging over my head."

Wynn said sweetly, "If you have a pencil close by, I can give you that amount now."

After a short pause, Aaron said, "Go ahead."

"Expenses of one hundred dollars for one set of decent bed linens and one set of decent men's pajamas."

"Yes? And the labor costs?" he asked in a dangerous tone.

"And three twenty-four-hour days at one dollar an hour for *childcare*. You're smart with money; you figure out what that comes to!" And before he could blast her eardrums with his reply, Wynn hung up.

By late Sunday afternoon Wynn felt well enough to leave her bed to lie on the couch in the living room and listen to Bach, so orderly and serene, on the stereo. She wore a pink and white striped challis nightgown, buttoned high around the neck, her cozy old pink velour robe, and not quite clean white bunny slippers on her feet.

When she heard the knock on the front door she thought it would be Lula, come to visit and, probably, to try to talk her out of exposing herself any further to the Bluebeard of the Penthouse. But when she opened the door, she was both amazed and embarrassed to see the devil himself. He was dressed in a way she'd never seen before, in a white turtleneck shirt that fit his torso so closely that little was left to the imagination regarding his musculature and tight, faded jeans that left even less regarding his masculinity. In his arms he carried a large picnic hamper and on his face he wore an uncertain smile.

"May I come in?"

"Oh! Well . . . I'm not dressed . . ."

"You saw me undressed for three days. One good turn deserves another," he said with a coaxing smile.

143

Wynn laughed. "All right, come in, I'll just go put something on."

"No, you can't do that," he protested with mock seriousness. "All modesty, propriety, and convention must bow to the natural law stating that when one is ill, one may not be dressed in day clothes."

At his words a little thrill of danger and excitement traveled up Wynn's spine. Pushing aside the memory of that episode in his sick-bed, Wynn laughed nervously and said, "Yes, that's right, now that you mention it." Besides, she told herself reassuringly, she was more covered up now, and swathed in more layers, than any of her day clothes afforded. Why be silly and coy? she asked herself, but uneasily. Aaron busied himself unloading the hamper and lining up its contents on the large round coffee table between the two love seats flanking the fireplace. An endless supply of snack foods appeared: herring in sour cream, a square loaf of sliced pumpernickel, a crock of chopped chicken liver, various boxes of imported crackers, a box of See's chocolate-covered cherries, peanut brittle, jellybeans, chunks of brie, Port Salut, Monterey Jack, Stilton, a loaf of San Francisco sourdough bread, crackling bags of potato chips, pretzels, and dried coconut flakes. From the bottom of the hamper he then retrieved a liter of white wine, and two six-packs, one of beer and one of a soft drink.

"I intended to invite myself for a meal," he explained, "and I didn't want to leave you an opening to say your larder was bare."

Scrambling mentally to think how she'd react to this event if it were anyone but Aaron, Wynn realized how very singular this man was to her. Imagine having to search for the proper response to what was, after all, a charming gesture of friendliness and good will from one person to another. Pretending that the devastating man standing expectantly in front of her was merely Ed Patterson or Jack or Paul, she smiled in what she hoped was a normal fashion and said, "How very nice of you; what a lovely surprise."

Looking closely at her, as if searching for a hidden barb, Aaron said off-handedly, "I would have invited you out, but Lula told me you were ill. I couldn't help feeling responsible . . ."

Blushing at his reference, and thinking back to her last telephone conversation with him when she'd hung up on him, Wynn said apprehensively, "You called Lula?" Surely he wouldn't be here if he'd called Lula to withdraw his proposition, would he?

"Yes, I called her to report your insubordination," he said sternly, but with a smile in his dark eyes. "But she begged me to forgive you. She assured me that you were deliriously ill, demented, raving, out of your mind, and not at all responsible for your words or actions."

Wynn lowered her eyes to hide her smile. "Well, yes, I was a bit under the weather that day."

An unspoken truce seemed to go into effect between them as they spent the next few hours together, eating an early supper, listening to records, sitting before the fire that Aaron built.

The fire had diminished into glowing coals when Aaron, in a lazy, comfortable voice, commented, "You know, this is a charming little house. You're fortunate that it's in a low-profile, middle-class, sort of backwater neighborhood. That will protect it from both trendiness and urban decay." Looking around him with a thoughtful, judicious expression, he added, "It's probably already worth a fortune. In the future, if you want to sell, you'll be able to write your own ticket."

Sitting beside Aaron on one of the love seats, encircled in his arms, a bit muzzy now from a full stomach and being out of bed too long, Wynn sleepily replied, "Do you ever think about anything but money?"

His arm tightened around her and he brushed his lips across her brow. "Oh, yes. Lately I do." Then, looking down at her face, he said, "Here, you're fading out on me. Let's get you to bed." He picked her up from the couch as if she were weightless.

With a noticeable lack of determination in her voice, Wynn protested that she'd see him out and get herself to bed. But he ignored her words and carried her from the room, saying, "What? And give up the one chance I may ever have to see *your* bedroom? After all, fair is fair."

He carefully set her down on the little antique rocking chair by her bed as he straightened out the sheets and plumped up the pillows. "Hmmm, I see you practice what you preach. *Your* sheets are very nice." Then he raised her to her feet, slowly untied the sash of her robe and let it fall to the floor around her feet. As Wynn looked up into Aaron's glowing, sable eyes, she felt mesmerized, paralyzed, like some small, helpless creature in the power of a strong force she could only hope would be beneficent.

As Aaron bent to kiss the hollow of Wynn's throat, he said huskily, "I want you to know I appreciate what you did for me when I was ill." His mouth moved up her slender neck to command her lips, and his kiss, lightly tender at first, deepened with each passing second until her lips opened to a welcoming oval that received and embraced the firm, yet gentle exploration of his tongue. His hand, like a warm spring breeze, drifted lightly into the opening of her gown and rested lightly on her trembling breast. A flood of such exquisite feeling poured through her that her knees buckled and she clutched Aaron's waist for support.

Embracing her now with both arms, Aaron pressed Wynn against himself, holding her hips close to him, closer still, as if he could make them one. When she felt the whole, hard length of him, felt his seductive heat against her body through the soft, thin cloth of her gown, Wynn moaned. She knew that she'd never want anything ever again as much as she wanted him to take her right now, on her bed, only inches away. Her arms, as if with a life of their own, rose like tendrils to wrap themselves around his firm body, to enclose him so he could never escape.

"Aaron," she whispered against his warm, searching lips, "Aaron . . . please . . ."

At the sound of his name Aaron loosened his embrace and took Wynn by the shoulders to steady her on her feet. Then, as if she were a small child, he buttoned up the neck of her gown, and, half-pushing, half-carrying her, he led her to her waiting bed. With a strangled laugh, his voice heavy and loose with passion, he whispered, "My, my, how you do carry on, Ms. Harris. What would your mother say?" And with a final chaste kiss on her brow, he left her tucked into bed like a child, and let himself out the front door.

In time the raging demands of her body lessened and Wynn lay between sleep and wakefulness, sometimes weeping, sometimes remembering, always wondering. *Why did he come? What does he think of me? Which Aaron—the tender one or the angry, suspicious one—is the real Aaron?*

Did his parting comment, "What would your mother say?" indicate that he still thought her a woman of loose morals? Did it indicate that he had never yet got over the circumstances of their first meeting, nor their second meeting when he saw her kiss Ed in public? And look at how she'd behaved with him, after all!

Then a disturbing new thought struck Wynn with sharp force: maybe she *was* loose! With him, she had been; how could she deny it? But how could she make her body resist him, when she loved him so?

Yes, in spite of everything—his stormy moods, his bad temper, his suspicious and cynical nature, his preoccupation with business and money, the fact that he wanted neither marriage nor children—Wynn admitted to herself that she loved Aaron Stone in just the way she'd always known she needed to love a man—the way her mother loved her father.

And what *would* Wynn's mother say? What would her mother think of her only child's falling in love with a thoroughly unsuitable man—a man who lived in the world of the arrogant and powerful rich, a man who disapproved of the work she did, who thought her loose and easy, who could never return her love in a million years— a man who might give her a month, six months, a year of joy as his new plaything, then turn away and leave her desolate. Wynn reached over to turn off her bedside lamp and settled down into her soft, warm bed, smiling serenely.

Her mother would approve.

CHAPTER THIRTEEN

During the following days Wynn did her best to separate her duties as Aaron's housekeeper from her personal feelings for him. Aaron, never an easy man at best, made it very difficult for her, one moment treating her as a close friend, the next as an employee—and more often than not—an unsatisfactory one. And sometimes, in spite of their care to avoid it, a moment of intimacy overwhelmed them both in the form of a stolen kiss or a caressing glance. During that first week she learned many things about the man who fascinated her so. He was a talented photographer, but fiercely private about this avocation. He was a superb cook, much better than Wynn ever hoped to be. And she saw that he was just as hard-headed as she'd always thought; but also, like so many cynics, he hid a soft and vulnerable heart, at least where his young nephews were concerned.

Many times during those early days Wynn thought back over the times when passion had flared between them, when he'd been tender with her, and wondered if it had meant any more to Aaron than a passing physical attraction or a means of showing her gratitude for what he saw as her kindness toward him when he was ill. Or perhaps those sweet moments that meant the world to her were merely a relaxing break in the monotony of his usual reserved, businesslike manner. So while her own feelings for the man deepened with daily proximity, her confusion as to his feelings for her grew no clearer.

At the beginning of this difficult new assignment Wynn had advertised for a permanent housekeeper in the city's two major newspapers as well as notifying all the employment agencies that handled skilled domestic workers. There had been a gratifying number of responses, but every applicant that Aaron interviewed had some fatal flaw that precluded hiring her. It didn't take Wynn long to understand that Aaron was sabotaging her every effort to replace herself and return to her own life. And yet, as each day in his company made it more difficult for her to separate her work from her feelings, Wynn continued to try to find the paragon he seemed to expect.

In the meantime she tried to make the awful penthouse more livable. She made small improvements such as replacing all the linens in the bedrooms and bathrooms and stocking the kitchen with normal staples. But try as she might, she couldn't make any headway on the basic dreariness of the place. In response to one of her veiled pleas to brighten the ambience of his home, Aaron replied with his usual cynicism. "I was raised in a house that was a decorator's dream. And in no corner of that showplace could a child find a crumb of laughter or love. It taught me that no amount of coordinated furniture and carpets and draperies could turn square footage into a home. I live here because it's close to my work, Wynn. That's all I expect of it. I don't give a damn what it looks like, and I'm not going to spend money on meaningless objects."

As the days wore on, the pressures in Wynn's life continued to escalate and converge. From the beginning of the assignment she'd spent her evenings and weekends at her own house—both to escape the daily tension of being close to and removed from Aaron, and because her own home needed care as well as his. There, one evening, she'd had a painful phone conversation with Ed Patterson in which he'd asked her, in his sweetly tentative way, to state her intentions toward him once and for all. Often, these days, Wynn asked herself if she should have destroyed all Ed's hopes, as she'd done. One day soon, mightn't she wake from this dreamworld, so full of pain and stress, to realize that she'd thrown away a life of happiness with a kind and solid man who loved her?

In addition, the month was drawing to a close and the time for Lula's decision drew ever nearer. If she decided against Aaron's offer to buy into Helpmates, she'd need to give him notice by the first of September. She'd have one month to find other funds and another location before the rent doubled on October first. Almost daily, by phone or in person, Wynn shared the distress that plagued Lula as she tried to come to a decision.

And worst of all, perhaps, Aaron grew more and more irascible. One memorable day Wynn had spent moving the heavy old furniture in the living room around in a vain attempt to bring a feeling of congeniality and warmth to the vast, dreary room. When Aaron came home that afternoon he stood in the foyer and looked about with a stormy look on his face.

"Just what do you think you're doing?" he demanded.

Physically exhausted and emotionally stung at his ingratitude, Wynn snapped back, "What do you care? I'm surprised you even noticed since you couldn't care less what this damn barn looks like!"

"If you can't leave well enough alone, I'd think you'd at least have the brains to call down for one of the maintenance men to help you with such heavy work," he said angrily. "I didn't hire you to be a furniture mover!"

"You hired me to be a housekeeper and I can't keep house in an airplane hangar! What's the point?" But he brushed past her and she didn't see him again until just before she left that evening when he sat down to the dinner she'd left prepared for him.

A few days later he came home unexpectedly early for lunch and caught her on her hands and knees scrubbing the huge tiled kitchen floor. He stood in the doorway scowling, his tall, taut body the very picture of towering anger. "Get up!" he ordered. "Look at your hands!"

Wynn sank back on her heels and looked up at him defiantly. "Why can't you leave me alone to do the work you hired me for!" she shouted back at him.

In three long strides he was upon her. Grasping her painfully by the upper arms, he yanked Wynn to her feet. "I won't have my . . . housekeeper doing that kind of heavy work. Why didn't you hire a cleaning person to do this? Are you deliberately trying to make me look bad?" he demanded, scowling.

Trying to wrest herself from his grip, Wynn looked around the kitchen and said sarcastically, "Look bad to whom? Do you see bleachers set up in here? Or maybe you're referring to the ghouls and ghosts that inhabit this mausoleum? And, besides, why should you look bad if I do an honest job of work for good pay!"

"You perverse little witch," Aaron muttered darkly, suddenly crushing Wynn to his chest with a force that took her breath away. Before she could protest, his lips covered hers angrily, his tongue thrusting itself forcefully into her mouth. In spite of the anger that was tantamount in Aaron's feelings for her at that moment, Wynn could neither still nor deny the excitement she felt at his touch. Even as she felt shamed that she responded to him under such circumstances, she felt her knees weaken and her body sag against him. Since she'd come to the penthouse to work for him she'd never understood why the sight of her working irritated him so; and she didn't understand why his anger today took the form of lovemaking, for no matter how rough and angry it was, there was no denying it was a sign of desire in this mysterious and troubled man.

"Aaron," Wynn murmured against his lips that angrily moved against hers, "you're hurting me . . ."

Instantly he loosened his grip on her, moaning, "Oh, sweet Wynn, I'm sorry. I don't want to hurt you, but you make me so angry."

After this humble speech Wynn expected to be released and was therefore all the more surprised when the result of her complaint was that Aaron quickly took off his suit jacket, tossed it on the damp floor, and kicked it into some semblance of a pillow. Then, as he kissed her face and neck with a gentle and persuasive passion, she felt the two of them sinking to the floor where Aaron carefully settled her head on the makeshift pillow.

As Wynn turned her head to accommodate the little kisses and nibbles Aaron was sprinkling on her ear and throat she saw the scrub bucket at eye level and the wet sponge oozing water where she'd left it when this remarkable scene began. But as his hand untied the large knot at her midriff and opened the gingham shirt to expose her naked breasts, Wynn's attention was drawn once again to the feelings coursing through her limbs at his touch. She felt his warm hands on her breasts, his palms feathering over her nipples until each was caught between gentle fingers and coaxed to hard points of desire.

In a swift, deft motion Aaron turned over to lie on the floor and rolled Wynn over to rest on the broad, hard plane of his chest. She settled herself blissfully into the delta of his thighs and felt his arousal grow to meet her own increasing need. With one free hand she stroked his long leg from hip to thigh, eliciting from him a strong, male groan.

"Does that give you pleasure, Aaron?" Wynn asked shyly.

He raised his head to look about him balefully, then lay back with a disgusted expression on his handsome face.

"At another time, no doubt it would—but I'm getting sopping wet from that damn sponge over there," he said.

With a feeling of terrible letdown, Wynn glanced over to see that the movements of their bodies had brought them within the sponge's puddle and Aaron's trouser bottoms were avidly soaking it up. With a laugh that sought to hide her humiliating predicament of being naked on a damp, half-scrubbed kitchen floor with a man who had once again turned peevish, Wynn moved quickly to release him.

But he held her fast, a serious, searching look in his eyes now. "First promise me something, Wynn, then I'll let you up."

"If I can," she said stiffly, knowing that just moments before she'd have promised him anything in the world.

"Never let me see you on your hands and knees again. I can't stand the sight of it."

With a demurring little smile Wynn's lashes dropped on her cheeks and she gave him a sort of shrugging nod. "I don't think I can promise that, Aaron. If I stay on this job very long, which I doubt, someday you may lose *all* your marbles and I might have to get down on my hands and knees to find the ones that roll under the furniture."

A few days later Anne called to say she was going shopping for Aaron's birthday gift that morning and would like to stop in for a cup of coffee if Wynn could spare the time. Wynn looked forward to the visit with the joyous expectation that a winter-bound pioneer woman might've looked forward to spring.

Glancing in the mirror beside the kitchen phone, Wynn saw with a jolt of surprise that in her general state of depression she'd let her hair get to a deplorably lank, limp state. In the maid's room she used during the day, she quickly rolled her long, black hair onto large pink rollers and sprayed her head with a setting lotion. Even a short time would give it some body, she thought. From there she returned to the kitchen to put a frozen coffee cake into the oven and brew a pot of coffee.

Aaron, rattling around somewhere in the far reaches of the penthouse, suddenly appeared with his camera in his hand. The fat pink rollers on her head brought an amused and tender smile to the sensual lips that had so often lately been drawn into a tight, unhappy line.

"You look like a Martian," he said lightly.

Wynn returned his smile, her embarrassment at being seen in this state overcome by her gladness at the welcome change in his mood. "Maybe I am!"

Still smiling, he sniffed the air. "I smell coffee. Do you have a spare cup before I leave?"

When he'd settled at the wrought iron table with his coffee, Wynn answered the bell of the oven timer and went to take the coffee cake out. As she bent over to open the door and reached in with a mitted hand, Aaron suddenly said, "Look at me and say cheese."

Startled, she raised her hand slightly as she raised her head, and the bright explosion of his flash went off at the same time as she felt the jolting pain of the oven's coils on her fingertips. With an anguished howl, she jerked back her hand, the coffee cake in its foil pan falling with a soft clatter to the floor.

In the instant Aaron was at her side, pushing her to the sink where he inundated her hand and the sleeve of her blouse as well in cold water from the tap. As the pain subsided, Wynn felt the comfort of Aaron's body pressing against her back and the security of his left arm as he held her body tightly while he bathed her right hand.

"I'm all right now," she said softly, a little breathless from his nearness and the pleasure of his concern.

So she was surprised when he growled in reply, "Look what you've done now, you clumsy little fool. Can't you ever be careful?"

Wynn went rigid and pulled away from him, her arm dripping water on the floor and her sleeve unpleasantly cold, plastered against her skin. "It was your fault, not mine! If you weren't constantly prowling around here with that damn camera of yours, startling me . . . What's the matter? Don't you have liability insurance? Are you afraid I'll sue you?" she said sarcastically.

Aaron stepped back from her and blinked in surprise. Then, his eyes narrowing, he said scathingly, "Look at yourself. Look at how rough and red your hands are. Look at the circles under your eyes. And now this! This can't go on, Wynn. This place is too much for you. Hire a cook. You're supposed to be a housekeeper, not a slave!"

With her mouth rounded in shock at this angry speech and her dark brown eyes open wide, Wynn stood defeated and watched Aaron stalk from the room. Seconds later she heard the front door slam shut.

Anne found her at the kitchen table in tears. A few kind, skillfully chosen questions were all it took for Wynn to pour her heart out to Aaron's warm-hearted, maternal sister.

"Oh, Anne, he's *right!* I really can't handle this job all alone and he won't let me hire anyone to replace me! I'm making a royal mess out of everything. I hate this place so much and I hate Aaron too! Oh, Anne, he's such a beast!" Wynn sobbed, unmindful that she was speaking of her friend's brother.

Anne patted Wynn's shoulder and crooned, "I know, dear Wynn. He can be very difficult, especially when his feelings are engaged. Would you like me to take over the screening of the housekeeper applicants? I won't even ask Aaron's approval. I'll just find someone to replace you and hire her myself."

Wynn's sobs ebbed to a moist sniffle as she looked at Anne in surprise. She hadn't realized how angry she had sounded, how Anne might interpret her words to mean that she wanted to leave Aaron. "Anne, it's very kind of you to offer, but I'll stick it out. I have to."

The day of Aaron's birthday was a busy one for Wynn. After a few days of angry silence between them, another truce had been called, and Wynn had agreed to accompany him that afternoon to help choose his gift to Anne, whose birthday was only a few days after his own. She was to be ready by three o'clock this afternoon, when he would leave the office and pick her up.

In the meantime she hurried to finish her own gift to him, the temerity of which now terrified her. She'd taken the liberty of entering Aaron's inner sanctum—the spare room where he stored his photographs and equipment—and selected a few of the most beautiful and moving of his pictures. She'd bought lucite do-it-yourself frames and intended to have them hanging on the living room walls when he arrived.

When they were all arranged and hung, Wynn was astounded at what they did for the room. She stood back and surveyed the artful photos: Anne's boys, heads together, both frowning over a broken toy truck; a tiny, wizened old Chinese man looking up in awe at an inhumanly beautiful, tall fashion model posing on Grant Avenue; an old, dilapidated Victorian house in the Haight-Ashbury district looming out of nowhere on a fog-shrouded street.

Surely he'll be pleased, she thought hopefully. But what if he wasn't? What if he thought she'd trespassed on his privacy, overstepped her bounds as an employee? With an unconscious gesture of despair, Wynn wrung her hands together. If only she knew what she was to him! In spite of his often sharp, angry words there were sometimes signs that he felt something for her. Punctually at three o'clock Aaron entered the penthouse foyer to find Wynn standing in the middle of the living room with an expectant, fearful look on her face. Her eyes riveted on him, she saw the first shock of surprise when he noticed the pictures, then, with a sinking heart, saw the protective shade she knew so well and dreaded so much close down over his expression and blank it out.

"Well," he said finally, "haven't you been the busy bee. When did you find the time to do all this?"

There was no way she could divine his feelings from his tone of voice. "Do you like them?" she asked hesitantly.

He cocked his dark head quickly to one side and shrugged. "You certainly picked out some of the better ones," he said grudgingly. "You have good taste, I'll give you that."

And with that damning with faint praise, Wynn had to be satisfied. Leery of pushing him any further for fear she'd hear a truth she didn't want to hear, she swallowed her disappointment and meekly walked to the foyer closet to put on her coat for their shopping trip.

On their way down in the elevator, trying to smooth things over, Wynn remarked casually, "It was Anne who told me your birthday was a few days before hers."

He turned to look at her with that unreadable expression still on his face, then replied without much interest, "Yes. Our father's tours always ended right before the Christmas season. He came home for the month of November." Then, after a short pause, he added in a sardonic tone, "Twice mother was unlucky and Anne and I were the results."

The past pain exposed by his remark went far toward healing Wynn's own hurt. His dreary, loveless childhood didn't excuse his every harsh word, of course, but it did perhaps explain why it was so hard for him to show whatever vulnerability he felt. Without another word Wynn slipped her arm into his and smiled tentatively up at the dark, brooding face. He glanced down at Wynn, briefly tightened his hold on her arm, and returned her smile with a small, dry smile of his own.

And so yet another truce was effected which might have lasted the day except for one unfortunate incident during the afternoon. Aaron took Wynn to Shreve & Company, one of the city's oldest and finest jewelry stores, on the corner of Post and Grant, to choose a pearl necklace for Anne. As the deferential salesman displayed a velvet tray of necklaces for Aaron's perusal, Wynn happened to glance across the room and saw, to her delight, Professor Jenkins at the diamond counter.

Not thinking of anything but her pleasure at seeing her favorite client, she left Aaron's side and hurried across the room to greet the professor with a glad cry. He looked in the absolute pink of health, his eyes now completely healed and sparkling with life. When he saw Wynn, his face flushed with a mixture of surprise, embarrassment, and pleasure. After giving her a warm hug, he turned back to the counter and waved vaguely over the brilliant gems.

"I was just . . . ah . . . looking these over, you see . . ."

Glancing behind her, Wynn saw Aaron standing stiffly where she'd left him, staring at her with that awful knowing smile she'd hated from the first time she'd seen it on his handsome face. As Wynn steered the professor over to meet Aaron she momentarily wondered why he'd behaved so guiltily at being seen looking at diamonds, but she had no need to wonder why Aaron looked as he did. All it took to bring that expression to his face was the sight of her with another man. If only it were something simple like jealousy, she thought in passing, instead of a relapse into his first impression of her as a woman of easy virtue.

After a short, uneasy introduction the professor made his apologies. "I really must run. I'm already late for an appointment." He took Wynn's hand in his and gently kissed it. "I do miss our evenings together, my dear. I'm

159

hoping for the pleasure of your company again in the near future."

Of all the possible remarks to make in the world, Wynn thought as she waved good-bye to him, that was without a doubt, the absolute worst.

Aaron finished making his purchase for Anne in grim silence. He grabbed Wynn's arm and marched her out of the store and headed in the direction of Chinatown, muttering that he wanted to pick up some trinkets for his nephews, if she thought she could spare the time.

Not even deigning to make a reply, Wynn tried to keep up with his angry stride as they walked the crowded, noisy, lively streets of the Chinese community. They passed small shops that sold exotic herbs, jade, silks, lacquer ware, with here and there a tourist trap that catered to the undiscriminating tourist who would accept any piece of junk at all so long as he could say it came from San Francisco's Chinatown.

They passed such a shop with a vivid gaudy display of T-shirts emblazoned with vulgar mottoes in its windows. Aaron jerked Wynn to a stop before this grimy shop window and pointed at a T-shirt within. "See that? I should buy that for you. It seems to be the story of your life."

Wynn focused where he pointed and read the yellow letters on a vile green background: SO MANY MEN—SO LITTLE TIME. A choke of rage rose in her throat. She turned to glare ferociously at him then whipped her head back to the display window and pointed to another shirt.

"No, you're wrong, as usual. *That's* the story of my life, and I'll buy it for myself!" She marched into the dank, dirty shop and paid a larcenous sum for an ugly purple shirt whose pink words said: A WOMAN WITHOUT A MAN IS LIKE A FISH WITHOUT A BICYCLE.

A venomous silence hovered between them all the way home, and as soon as Wynn entered the penthouse she went to the maid's room to change out of her lovely pink and lavender tweed suit into the ugly T-shirt and her jeans. As she haphazardly threw a makeshift dinner together for Aaron prior to going home—for she'd secretly hoped he'd take her out for dinner to celebrate his birthday—she wore the tacky shirt while fervently hoping and praying that she'd insulted him so severely that he'd never, ever recover. Wynn's movements were jerky and clumsy with righteous indignation as she warmed up a plate of leftover macaroni and cheese in the microwave oven and tossed a slightly wilting lettuce salad with bottled dressing. Aaron leaned against the kitchen door jamb, his arms crossed rigidly over his chest and glowered silently at her. Wynn plunked the food on a silver tray and brushed past him on her way to the dining room where she set his place at the head of the long, empty table.

Passing him by again on her way to the maid's room to collect her clothing, she said loftily, "Dinner is served, sir."

With her jacket on and her suit and blouse over her arm Wynn had to walk through the wide hallway to reach the foyer, and from there she couldn't avoid seeing Aaron sitting forlornly at the table in the cavernous dining room, picking listlessly at the nearly inedible food she'd served him. Hating herself for it, but unable to leave without at least a word of good-bye, she called to him, "I'm leaving now."

She'd nearly reached the front door when she heard the clatter of silverware on china behind her, and within seconds he was upon her in the foyer, gripping her upper arm and turning her roughly to face him. "You're not going out on the street in that ridiculous get-up!" he growled.

Wynn's eyes narrowed in fury. "Don't worry, no one will know I work for the eminent Aaron Stone. They'll just think I'm a hooker. That's what *you* think, isn't it?"

Aaron's face darkened to a frightening degree and in reply he yanked Wynn to him and kissed her with bruising force. "I'll show you what I think," he muttered. Pushing her against the foyer door, he snatched her suit and blouse from her arm and tossed them to the floor. Then, with angry, impatient motions, he roughly divested her of her jacket. Alarmed now, Wynn pushed against his chest with all her strength, but his superior size coupled with his angry determination rendered her best efforts useless.

"Let me go!" she gasped, but his only reply was to capture her mouth with his while his hands roamed her body like vandals. There was a force in him that both frightened and thrilled her, as if a need too long denied was rampant at last. When he tore the hairpins from her hair and raked his fingers through the long tresses, Wynn thought yearningly of that first time he'd done the same thing, but so gently, so tenderly. Crushed against the hard door as she was, nearly stifled by his hard body against the length of hers, his hands marauding now under the insulting T-shirt, instead of caressing as they once had, his lips hard and punishing instead of searching and seeking, Wynn felt hot tears of anguish and loss burn in her eyes.

If only he could love me as I love him! But every move he now made proved him incapable of such a tender emotion and the truth of this realization so devastated Wynn that her whole body sagged and slackened against him in hopeless defeat. At this signal of submission, Aaron loosened his iron grip for a split second, moving his head back to gaze at Wynn's tear-streaked face. At the sight of the misery in her face, Aaron groaned from deep within himself. "Oh, no, what am I doing to you when I want only to make you happy—to make us both happy."

Wynn was so startled at his words that she doubted she'd heard him correctly. Never since she'd known him had she heard him make such an intimate and obviously sincere remark. "Aaron?" she questioned joyfully, lifting her hand to caress his face. He seized her hand and hungrily kissed her palm, then enfolded her body to his in a warmly encompassing embrace. The touch of his lips on hers now was soft and deep, his tongue thrusting within the moist, sweet welcome of Wynn's mouth.

As if she were weightless, Aaron picked her up in his arms. As she twined her arms around the sinewy column of his neck and rested her face against the firm muscles of his chest, she felt the hard, excited beating of his heart answer the fluttering sensation in her own breast. She felt herself being transported both physically and emotionally as he walked through the large living room and down the hall to his bedroom. With each step Aaron took, Wynn's desire for him increased until her body was one clamoring cry for fulfillment. Aaron lowered her to the bed and sat close beside her, never taking his hands from her for a second, as if, Wynn thought, smiling privately, he actually thought she had the strength to refuse now what she'd waited for so long.

Gently pulling the offensive T-shirt over Wynn's cloud of hair, Aaron said in a voice rough with passion, "We don't need this now—and *you* will never need it again."

When the shirt was discarded on the floor beside the bed, Aaron's fingers moved with a firm assurance to unzip Wynn's jeans and maneuver them down her hips and off to join the shirt. Kneeling over her now, he gazed down at her nearly naked body with an expression of slumberous awe. In a voice thick with desire he murmured, "How exquisitely beautiful you are."

Burning to see Aaron in all his beauty too, Wynn now smiled languorously and reached up to unbutton the dress shirt he still wore, then began to pull it in gentle tugs from his tightly belted waistline.

"Let me help you, darling," Aaron said huskily, but Wynn stopped his move to hasten his own undressing.

"No, I want to do it," Wynn said shakily. As she removed the stiff white shirt from the smooth, swarthy, gracefully muscled torso, she trembled at the sight of such perfect beauty hiding under his traditional, unassuming clothes.

Wynn wouldn't have thought it possible to want him more than she already did, but after he'd whispered away with magical fingers her bra and panties, after he'd stroked her abdomen and thighs in some arcane pattern all his own, after he'd caressed her naked body from fingertips to toes, kissing and tasting as if he could never get enough of her, she gasped out her desire for him, writhing and quivering beneath him. "Oh, Aaron, I want you, I want you now," she groaned, reaching up to pull him closer to her, ready to be one with him.

With the speed of passion too long restrained, Aaron unbuckled his belt and with Wynn's eager help divested himself of all barriers between himself and her. Wynn gazed in awe at the sight of his magnificent body in all its manly power, and the knowledge that she was the cause of his arousal thrilled her more than she'd believed possible. It gave her a feeling of feminine power she'd never known but now would never forget.

Aaron lowered himself to cover Wynn's waiting body and at the touch of his smooth skin against her sensitive, aroused flesh, she felt a flash of flame that she knew only Aaron could extinguish. "I want you too, my beautiful Wynn. I've wanted you from the first time I saw you," he whispered, his dark, wavy hair nestled in the hollow of her neck. So natural was it, so much what she'd wanted for so long, although she'd denied it, that at first she felt only the sweet, heavy fullness deep within her. Clutching Aaron's torso with her arms, cradling his hips within her legs, she felt her heart and soul open to him as joyfully as her body. In the maelstrom of her surging emotions, while the world of reality faded away, every detail of their coupling stood out in brilliant detail: the almond scent she'd grown to associate only with Aaron, the crisp mat of hair that rubbed against her own swollen breasts, the sinewy muscles of his back and the tautness of his buttocks, the heavy rasp of his breath that proved his excitement was as frantic as her own.

It was only when the rhythmic, rocking movements began that the delicious sensations spread from her core to all the boundaries of her body in ever-widening, ever-deepening waves until she was lifted out of herself and, with a cry of joyous triumph, reached and bypassed the exquisite peak of earthly delight to steal a touch of heaven. From the heights he'd taken her to, her whole body open and receptive to joy now, Wynn reveled again and yet again when Aaron too cried out in fulfillment, and, shuddering once, collapsed in contentment beside her. Still drugged by the searing heat of her body, Wynn dreamily noticed that the room was dim now, lit only by the twilight. Aaron's head lay heavily on her arm, his left hand stroking her flat stomach. She twirled the dark waves of his hair with her fingers and sighed.

At the satisfied sound Aaron propped himself up on one elbow and studied her relaxed face, tracing it with his fingertips, memorizing her lips, her eyes, her chin. They exchanged a slow, sweet, intimate kiss. His hand moved down Wynn's legs and stroked her. Wynn felt the passion building all over again.

"You're marvelous, Wynn—so giving, so warm. The way you respond to me makes me want you over and over and over again. When I think of all the time we wasted while I watched you move the furniture and scrub the floor . . ."

CHAPTER FOURTEEN

For a second, Wynn lay still, her mind racing. Then she removed Aaron's hand, turned on the bedside lamp, and stared at his dark, handsome face still softened with passion. "What do you mean by that?" she asked in a colorless, waiting tone.

Even in the dusky light she saw his lean cheeks redden. He rolled away from her onto his back and covered his eyes with the back of his hand. His voice was still husky with content as he replied. "Nothing. Just what I said. It was wonderful for me—and for you, too, I thought. You're a wonderful lover." Removing his hand from his eyes, he turned to look at her. "I know what you're thinking. It was a stupid thing to say under the circumstances, I admit. But I swear I didn't mean it the way it . . . may have sounded."

How quickly he'd known what she referred to! How quick he was to deny even before she accused! And there was no ring of truth in his voice for her to cling to. Wynn sat up, reaching for her clothes on the floor by the bed. Her nakedness was an exposure now, a mortifying shame, when just seconds before it had been a glorious gift, a source of the purest joy she'd ever known in her life.

"Hey, what are you doing?" Aaron asked as Wynn hastily pulled on her clothes. "I thought we'd agreed that you wouldn't need that awful shirt again," he said, trying

to inject a note of levity into his voice. Then, more seriously, he added, "I thought we'd go out to dinner . . ."

"To celebrate your conquest?" she said bitterly, barely
able to speak over the painful lump in her throat. "To
celebrate your initiation into the club of *all my men?* Well,
no thanks," she threw over her shoulder as she hurried out
of the bedroom into the living room. "As a matter of fact,
you still don't qualify for membership!"

Hastily zipping up the trousers he'd thrown on to follow
her into the living room, Aaron said caustically, "Oh?
And just what does it take to join that august body?"

"Forget it. Whatever it takes, you don't have it."

She admitted to herself now that she'd been waiting for
him to say it all during their lovemaking. If he'd said a
simple "I love you," she could have believed that his
"compliment" about her lovemaking was just that—a
light and loving remark from one lover to another. But he
hadn't said it and he never would. His remark proved that
his original opinion of her still hadn't changed. And his
embarrassment and denial only served to prove it. Wynn's
heart ached that this man she'd given so much of herself
to had succeeded in making her feel as low and be-
smirched as he thought her to be.

Just then the phone rang in Aaron's study and his voice
on the answering machine could clearly be heard from
where the two of them stood in the huge, dark room,
avoiding each other's eyes. At the end of the beep they
heard Lula Dobbs's voice identify herself and say, "Mr.
Stone, I've decided I can't accept your terms. I'm sorry to
let all my people down, but it just wouldn't be worth my
while to be a junior partner in my own business. However,
thanks for your offer."

Wynn heard the pathetically dignified message with a
sinking heart. She thought of all the hard work gone for
naught, the people out of work, and Lula's blasted hopes.

"I'm leaving now," she said, repeating her words of such a short time ago.

"Please, don't go just yet. We should talk." He gestured toward the room from where the message had come. "There may be other alternatives we haven't explored . . ."

Even though there was a humble tone she'd never heard before in Aaron's voice, Wynn was too heartsick to give it much credence. She'd been playing out of her league all along, she realized now. He really was a shark, and fool minnow that she was, she'd best escape before she lost everything—in addition to her heart.

As she walked toward the door, she turned to smile sadly at him and gestured to the photographs she'd hung on the bare walls with such hope of pleasing him. "You didn't like your birthday present at all, did you?"

"Is that why you did it? Because you thought I'd dislike it?" he asked quietly.

Wynn shook her head. "No, they're very beautiful. You really should consider having an exhibition."

"Then why did you do it?"

Something in his flat tone, in the self-assured stance of his body, in the arrogance of his choice of conversation when Wynn's whole world lay in shatters at her feet, released a tightly closed lid on a roiling well of rage that now exploded with the force of a volcano.

"I did it to please you! I did it because this place is so big and so ugly and so empty! I did it because I hate it here and I wanted to give it some beauty and some life!"

Aaron started to walk toward her. In a conciliatory tone, he said, "Oh, all right, if you hate it so much, then go ahead and hire a decorator."

Clenching her fists at her side, Wynn backed away from him and said furiously, "That's always your solution, isn't it? *Hire* someone. Hire a cook. Hire a furniture pusher. Hire a cleaning person. Now, at long last, it's hire a decorator! You don't need a housekeeper, you need a personnel manager!"

Wynn turned to leave, then, remembering Lula, she stopped and whirled to accuse him. "And one more thing! When you might have done something meaningful with your pots of money, instead of just using it to hire out your whole life for other people to live for you, you could have made Lula a loan she could've lived with. Even if her business is chancy, don't you have enough money to take a chance? But no! You had to make an employee out of her too!"

"I wanted to make a partner of her!" Aaron protested.

"Some partner!" Wynn retorted. "What chance would she have had with you and that ice maiden teamed up against her, holding fifty-one percent of the power? Well, your greedy scheme didn't work, did it? And I hope it's taught you something—that she'd rather go out of business than be beholden to *you*. And that goes for me too. From now on, you can hire people to do for you till hell freezes over! I quit!"

In two long, catlike strides, Aaron caught Wynn on her way to the door and spun her around, his face taut and white with anger. "So you're quitting, are you?" he said scornfully. "Is that supposed to come as a surprise? I never did fall for all that phony talk of yours about the nobility of wifehood and how what was good enough for your mother was good enough for you. You're just like all the others—only too glad to accept all the benefits of marriage but refusing to put up with any of the drawbacks —sniveling when the going gets rough . . . backing out . . . *quitting!*"

In a cold fury Wynn retorted, "Now, just a minute. My quitting has nothing whatever to do with my feelings about love or marriage. You're an employer and I'm an employee—that's all we are to each other. In a marriage there are such things as love and loyalty and commitment.

Many things can be and are overlooked. But we're not talking about marriage here, we're talking about a job. We're talking about working conditions—not about love!"

In a sad, dreary voice, Wynn added, "There's no love here."

"You can certainly say that again," Aaron agreed coldly. "So why don't you just remove yourself from these unsatisfactory working conditions and go back to your cozy, valuable little cottage where you can scrub floors and hang up pictures to your solitary little heart's content."

"Just watch my dust," Wynn muttered, her solitary heart breaking within her as she slammed the penthouse door behind her.

Helpmates had the month of September still to run on its lease, but Lula was filling assignments only for old customers, so Wynn and the others had a lot of time on their hands to seek other work.

One day in the middle of the month Wynn had lunch with Anne, at Anne's request. She had a friend who was soon to undergo a serious major operation and Anne was collecting blood donors for her. Wynn was glad to be able to help the kind young woman whose acquaintance she'd hoped would grow into friendship. When Wynn didn't ask about Aaron, Anne didn't volunteer any information. Wynn was grateful that Anne was sensitive enough to know the very mention of her brother's name would open a wound in Wynn that showed no signs of healing.

Near the end of the month Wynn invited Lula to lunch at her house, so they could have a nice, long, private chat. When her guest arrived, Wynn was surprised to see her looking so rested and relaxed. She wore a more subdued costume than usual, a pretty pastel yellow suit with a blouse to match in a restrained floral pastel print.

Too depressed to cook, Wynn had ordered lunch in

from the excellent caterer whose wares she'd taste-tested so long ago at Aaron's dining table. While she and Lula ate the exquisite quenelles, Lula brought Wynn up-to-date on all she'd missed during those fruitless days she'd wasted in the penthouse.

"I hope you'll be as happy as I am to hear that my Meg and Ed Patterson are engaged to be married, Wynn, dear," Lula said gently.

Wynn assured her that she couldn't be happier; and it was true. She wanted nothing more for Ed than to find the happiness he yearned for, the happiness that she could never have given him—and now could never give to anyone. For she knew that Aaron Stone had been the one man in the world she could have loved in the way she needed to love with all her heart and soul and being.

It seemed that cupid had been working overtime at Helpmates, for Paul too had a lady love. "And you'll never guess who she is!" Lula chortled. "Her daddy is a Texas neurosurgeon with interests in oil and real estate, as rich as Croesus, my dear. He met her while tending bar at a medical party given by Jack Clancey's woman doctor client while the AMA convention was in town. Can you imagine our Marxist marrying an heiress? Isn't it rich?"

Wynn laughed at the rationalizations Paul would have to go through to explain his marrying a capitalist. "Love will find a way," she joked.

It was while they were having coffee and dessert that Wynn got to the real point of her invitation. She handed Lula a check for a very large amount of money made out to Lula Dobbs and signed by Wynn Harris.

"But my dear girl! Where did you get so much money?" Lula cried.

Wynn explained that she couldn't bear it that Lula should go out of business simply for lack of money, so she'd mortgaged her house. "I own it outright, you know.

The money was just sitting there, doing nobody any good. I can't imagine why I didn't think of it weeks ago."

Lula's bright blue eyes gleamed with tears. "What an angel you are, Wynn. But I can't accept it. I don't need it anymore."

Wynn insisted, protesting that she must take it, but Lula held up a well-manicured, soft hand, and with a shy smile showed Wynn the modest diamond on the ring finger.

"Who?" Wynn asked breathlessly.

"Roger Jenkins," Lula replied with a delighted laugh. "And this is thanks to you, too, Wynn. I'd met him when he first came to Helpmates, of course, but it wasn't until you called in sick that day that I really got to know him. I took your assignment myself that night. The rest is history. Isn't he wonderful, Wynn?" Lula asked shyly.

"Oh, yes, he is. But remember what you said that day about working for other people all your life even during your marriage to Harry? Lula, are you sure you want to give up your business to marry? You can easily have both now."

But Lula insisted she was sure. She and Roger had talked it over and when he retired in two years they wished to do a lot of traveling. There were many plans in the air and they both wanted to be free and unfettered.

"If you're sure, then I simply couldn't be happier for you," Wynn said sincerely.

"You might like to know that you're the second person within the week to offer me a great sum of money, Wynn. Aaron Stone came to me the day after I left my message on his machine and made me a new offer of a loan at less than current rates, with no strings attached. He even made sure to explain that he'd had to double all the rents in the building because the property was reassessed for the first time since he'd bought it and the taxes doubled. He couldn't have been nicer, Wynn. I just thought you might be interested in knowing he's not a complete monster."

"Yes, I knew that already," Wynn said with a pang of remembrance for all the sweet times she'd known with the man of stone.

Later that evening, alone in her house, Wynn looked about her at the comfortable nest she'd fashioned for herself. She'd promised she'd be maid of honor at Lula's wedding to Roger Jenkins, and soon she'd have two more weddings to attend, unless funny, crazy Paul had an extravaganza somewhere in the wilds of Texas. But in the meantime, and for the foreseeable future, here sat Wynn Harris with no family, no intimate companion, no love.

All she had was a roof over her head and a very large sum of money that needed to be looked after. Just like Aaron Stone.

CHAPTER FIFTEEN

October was a frantic month for Wynn and she welcomed every busy moment that kept her stubborn heart from brooding pointlessly over Aaron Stone. As she sat in the new home of Helpmates Inc., ready to begin another full day, she pondered the events that had so quickly brought her to a success she'd never have dreamed of a few short weeks ago.

It seemed to her that she'd made very few changes, really. She advertised now in the neighborhood shopping flyers instead of the much more expensive ads in the city's large newspapers, the *Chronicle* and the *Examiner*. She'd wrangled an interview on several local TV magazine shows to publicize the business. Since so much in housewifery defied description and was so difficult to evaluate, Wynn now charged a flat hourly fee rather than charging by the individual task as Lula had done.

The basic improvement in her positive cash flow came, of course, from capitalizing herself with the mortgage money she'd originally borrowed for Lula. Now that she ran the business from her own home, and lived there as well, the fixed mortgage payment was her only monthly outlay for both her working space and her living space. Wynn had never thought it necessary for a business like Helpmates to be housed in a prime location anyway. She was fortunate that the city's zoning regulations allowed a low-traffic business such as hers in this "backwater" neighborhood. Now, instead of a slick, hokey country kitchen in a high-rise office building, Wynn had what she'd always had: a comfortable, charming house. Most of her clients contacted her by phone anyway, and the few who liked to drop by could easily find parking space in this residential area.

As she sat at the pretty little desk she'd moved from her bedroom to the living room bringing last week's records up-to-date, Wynn felt bemused that she, the young woman who had no other ambition than to marry and have a family, who'd intended only to mark time with an interesting job perfecting the skills she'd expected to use in her personal life, should be fast developing into a successful businesswoman—more by default than by design.

When the old-fashioned shop bell she'd fixed to her front door suddenly jingled, Wynn looked up with an expectant, businesslike smile on her face. The smile slid away when she saw, framed in her doorway, the sorely missed and much wept over Aaron Stone. His expression was somber, and under his arm he carried a large, flat parcel wrapped in brown paper and grocery string.

"I've come to inquire about hiring a wife. Have I come to the right·place?"

Although her heart was dancing madly with the joy of seeing him, Wynn had by no means forgotten his power to cause her great pain. Her expression was bland and her voice was cool as she replied, "Yes, indeed. We have the best wives for hire that money can buy. You do have money, I trust?"

A slight reddening colored the taut skin over Aaron's high cheekbones. "Oh, yes, ma'am, money is the one thing I have plenty of." He lowered the large parcel to the floor, then, indicating the client's chair in front of the desk, he asked permission with his liquid, glowing eyes to sit down. When Wynn nodded, Aaron settled himself into the chair, crossed his long legs, and leaned back with his arms crossed over his chest. Gratefully recognizing that he wished to keep this confrontation on a business basis, Wynn too leaned back in her chair, hiding her eagerness to hear what he had to say.

"Now, then," he began gravely, "not just any wife will do, you understand. My requirements are precise and particular. She must be brilliant, black-haired, and beautiful. Shall I go on? Or do I have you stumped already."

Even though Aaron spoke with a straight face, Wynn detected a vulnerable look in his dark eyes that touched her but not enough to make her lower her guard.

"That depends," Wynn replied, matching his serious tone. "What duties did you have in mind? There are certain kinds of . . . work . . . we don't do here, you know."

Aaron smiled briefly at this comment and nodded his understanding. "I need an all-around wife, so to speak, a Jill-of-all-trades, and mistress of one."

"I see. And that one trade she must be mistress of?"

Aaron lowered his eyes. "Well, that may be the most difficult requirement of all; it's so rare. She'd have to be mistress of the difficult task of loving a blind and neurotic fool."

Masking her face to hide the leap of joy she felt in her heart at this oblique admission of fault from this proud man, Wynn pretended to take notes, then inquired, "And what is the approximate duration of this assignment? How many hours of work do you require? We charge a flat hourly fee, you understand."

In a lighter, more natural voice, Aaron said, "Thank God you asked, after I went to so much trouble to figure it out on my calculator. I need her for three hundred ninety four thousand, two hundred hours. That takes me up to my eightieth birthday. After that, well, we'll see how it's working out."

Wynn couldn't help laughing at this charming nonsense, but she quickly resumed her previous role of interviewer. "I'm afraid I can't help you until I have a more detailed idea of your needs. Can you define the duties of this wife more clearly?"

Aaron cleared his throat and took a deep breath. "Well, for one thing, I've just divested myself of a business partner of many years standing, and I need a wife who might be interested in filling that role eventually. I need a wife who will complement my own qualities rather than simply reinforcing them. For instance, I have a tendency to be rather hard and cynical, I'm afraid, and I need a wife who can soften these qualities. Then, too, I have a somewhat voracious talent for making money, and I need a wife who can balance that with a concern for the human element."

Wynn said softly, "You seem to have a fair understanding of your own nature. That's not usual in most businessmen, if you'll pardon my saying so."

"Yes. Well, I've just recently learned these things the hard way. But perhaps that's the only way to learn, when one is as stupid and blockheaded as I've been."

At these humble words Wynn felt the love and longing for him, so harshly repressed and denied these past weeks, burgeoning within her again, like a bud whose time to bloom has come and will not be denied. Everything in her yearned to reach out to him, to touch him, to give him anything and everything he wanted. But in spite of the impressive change he seemed to have undergone, the important words had still not been said. He'd said he needed a wife to love him in spite of his faults, but he hadn't said he needed to love a wife.

Wynn's shoulders slumped and she lowered her so recently eager eyes and said sadly, "I'm very sorry, but I don't believe we have anyone to fit your precise and particular needs here. Perhaps you'll have better luck elsewhere."

Aaron's face tightened with anxiety. "Come now! You're just not trying! Here, maybe if I give you more to go on." He stood up and retrieved the parcel from the floor, ripped off the paper and held it up for Wynn to see. It was a picture of herself, a black-and-white blowup in poster size. She saw herself in three-quarter-face view, her black hair done up in fat rollers, looking at the camera with a startled, questioning gaze as she reached into the oven with both hands. In the bottom right hand corner of the white mat that framed the poster was the title: HELP-MATE.

Tears came to Wynn's eyes as she remembered the events surrounding that picture. She remembered the camaraderie just before it, the pain just a split second after the flash, and the humiliation when she'd mistaken his annoyance with her clumsiness for concern.

But the picture and Aaron's presence here today—the change in him—could they be evidence that she was wrong? Was she perhaps expecting the leopard to change too many spots all at once? And, after all, did she want so many changes in the man she'd fallen in love with just as he was?

Wynn's question was partially answered when Aaron rushed to her where she still sat behind the desk, raised her from her seat, and took her into his arms. "Oh, my darling Wynn, please don't tell me to look elsewhere for my dearly beloved wife," he whispered huskily. "If I can't have you, then no one else in the world will do."

Involuntarily Wynn clung to him, the strength and warmth of his body so close to hers again, filling her with deep satisfaction, like a parched throat slaked with cool, life-giving water. She raised her tear-wetted face to his, and he covered her waiting lips with his hungry mouth, crushing her to him as if he'd never again let her go. Wynn felt the love within her soar and build into a spiral of desire that she knew need never again be denied.

Putting her gently from him, so he could look into her eyes, Aaron asked urgently, "Can you ever forget what an idiot I've been, my darling? Can you forgive what I've put you through?"

"Oh, Aaron," Wynn breathed tremulously, "if you love me I can forgive you anything . . ."

"If I love you!" he moaned. "Can you doubt it? Have you ever doubted it?"

"A time or two," Wynn said slyly, burying her face in his broad, warm chest, inhaling that wonderful almond aroma of his person. With a quiver of delight she felt the rumble of his laugh reverberate through her body.

But even now, still feeling the anguish his doubts had caused her, Wynn fell serious again. "Such as all those times you thought I was . . . for hire. Even when we made love, when you said that's what I was good at . . ." she whispered sadly, needing to hear him deny those painful charges, even as she'd begun to believe he loved her.

Aaron held her loosely now, his cheek resting on the gleaming black cushion of her hair. "How can I explain it to you," he said softly, "when I scarcely understand it myself." He was quiet for a moment, urgently stroking Wynn's shoulders, her bare arms, her throat, her breasts, unaware, in his thoughtful distraction, of the burning responses his caresses evoked in Wynn's sensitive, loving body. Then finally he sighed heavily.

"You were simply too good to be true," he said thoughtfully. "I think that's what it was, at first. I just couldn't believe that a woman like you still existed—a warm, beautiful, capable woman, a woman of loyalty and integrity, and hardest of all for me to believe was that a woman like that, with talent and independence, actually wanted to marry and have a family."

Wynn softly began to protest, as she once had to Professor Jenkins, that she was not so rare as he thought, when Aaron stopped her words with a soft, quick kiss, and continued. "And then, as time went on, and I grew to know you were truly what you seemed to be, I couldn't believe that you could ever care for a sour, twisted misanthrope like myself."

"But, my darling!" Wynn protested, indignant that anyone, even supposedly herself, could presume to not adore the man she'd adored in silence for so long. "I loved you from that very first moment in the restaurant although, I admit, I didn't realize it for quite a while, charming though you were," she finished with teasing sarcasm.

Her heart quickened at the sight of that boyish grin on the usually stern man's face. "Yes, I admit I was often at my most charming with you," he said, meeting her sarcasm with his own. Then, seriously, he explained, "You brought out the worst in me, I admit. I felt driven to push you to the limit, to test you, to find out for sure that you were what I so desperately wanted you to be. I had to make sure you weren't responding to me—the few times you did respond—for Lula's sake. Or just because I was wealthy."

He groaned then and pulled Wynn close to him, pressing her hips against him, showing her with his body as well as his words that he wanted her with all his vulnerable, masculine heart.

"And will you ever forgive me for the way I botched Lula's business?" he asked sincerely.

Wynn told Aaron that she knew of the amends he'd tried to make, and she added, "Besides, you were right all along, basically. Even I could see the ways dear Lula was mishandling the business. And I think you'll agree that the changes I've made are all for the good. The business will grow as it should now." Then Wynn added teasingly, "Maybe if you treat me nicely, I'll let you become *my* business partner some day."

Aaron smiled down at her, his dark eyes warm with love. "Helpmates is your baby, for now, my love. If you want a partner in the future, we'll talk about it. But for now I only want your promise that you'll be my very own, exclusive helpmate, starting tonight."

Wynn laughed exultantly. "Now you're asking the impossible! If you want to make an honest woman of me, that is!"

Aaron laughed and covered her face with a flurry of sweetly impatient kisses. The touch of his hand firmly cupping the back of her head to pull her closer to him, to hold her within the circle of his arms, began to work its magic on Wynn, and she knew that, legal or not, if Aaron wanted her tonight, it couldn't be soon enough. But then from the inner pocket of his jacket he took a piece of official-looking paper and handed it to her. It was a license to marry, made out in their names.

"But how?" And then Wynn remembered the trip to the hospital a few days ago to have her blood typed for Anne's friend, and a mulish look came over her face. Not sure whether to laugh or to complain that Aaron had manipulated her again, she opened her mouth to protest, but he stopped her with a kiss.

"No, it's not what you're thinking," he said, grinning. "There really is a sick friend, and, by the way, I love you for being willing to help her. I just took the opportunity that presented itself, that's all."

Then with a wry smile, he confessed, "Yes, the opportunity to box you in, to cut off any possibility of second thoughts, or escape. I wanted to trap you so that we can marry in haste and repent at leisure. Have I succeeded?"

In her exultant, grateful heart, Wynn now knew that the man she loved so completely returned her love, that she'd exceeded the limit of human joy and succeeded in stealing a touch of heaven to keep for her own the rest of her life.

Wynn's eyes gleamed with tears of love as Aaron strode hastily to the front door and flipped the CLOSED sign on the front door and locked it. So urgent was their need for each other that they left a trail of clothes behind them from the living room to Wynn's bedroom. There, in the dim light of the room they faced each other, holding hands and gazing on each other like the first lovers of the world.

Aaron drew Wynn toward him and encircled her silken body within one arm while with the other hand he loosened the black fall of her hair to the petal-soft skin of her shoulders. He firmly encircled her rib cage and pressed up to lift her breasts to his hot, searching mouth, delicately tasting first one sensitive, erect nipple, then the other with the warm moisture of his tongue.

Wynn draped her trembling arms around Aaron's naked shoulders and slid them down the full, hard, sinewy length of his body, then raised herself onto her tiptoes to press his hips deep against her own thighs. When the desperately desired contact was made, they groaned together and, as one body, sank onto the bed clasped in each other's arms.

Aaron's dark, wavy hair hovered over Wynn's soft curves now, his mouth moving like a fiery brand over breasts and navel and her electrifyingly sensitive thighs. Where his mouth forged the way, his fingertips followed, probing in little circles of loving, maddening pressure into the deep core of her body.

"Aaron," she cried out, gasping for the release her tantalized body hungered for. "Take me now, my darling!"

"I want it to go on forever," Aaron groaned, the musky smell of almonds nearly drugging Wynn as he moved his moist, hot skin to cover hers. "But I can't wait either, my sweet, sweet Wynn."

Wynn slipped her open palm between their clinging hips and stroked his lithe, taut thighs one last delicious time before she felt the sudden, wished-for merging of his body with hers. His strong arms held her up under the hips, the better to give her pleasure, and as he moved first gently, then more and more forcefully, she felt herself rising higher and higher to meet him until there was nothing in the world but Aaron and his love and the pleasure only he could give her. They reached the peak together, both crying out as the exquisite sensations spiraled to a crescendo that was nearly painful in its power.

Their bodies sated, they gently separated like two parts of a ripe fruit, and lay breathing quietly into the still electric air of the room. Aaron moaned with deep satisfaction, then raised himself up on one elbow and gazed down into his beloved's face. Wynn reached up to urge his dark head down to her waiting mouth, and looked up into his eyes that glowed with love. She smiled blissfully up into the face she knew she'd never tire of, the face she'd love above all others for the rest of her life, content to know whose wife she'd been tonight.

LOOK FOR NEXT MONTH'S
CANDLELIGHT ECSTASY ROMANCES™

When You Want A Little More Than Romance—

Try A Candlelight Ecstasy!

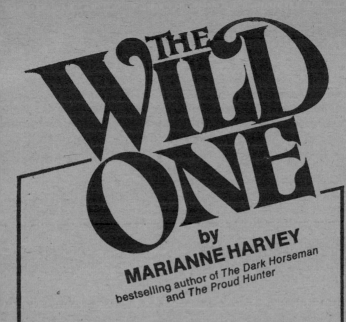

THE WILD ONE

by
MARIANNE HARVEY
bestselling author of *The Dark Horseman*
and *The Proud Hunter*

Proud, beautiful Judith—raised by her stern
grandmother on the savage Cornish coast—
boldly abandoned herself to one man and sought
solace in the arms of another. But only one man
could tame her, could match her fiery spirit,
could fulfill the passionate promise of rapturous,
timeless love.

A Dell Book $2.95   (19207-2)

"THE MOST ROMANTIC NOVEL SINCE LOVE STORY."
—Good Housekeeping

Change of Heart

SALLY MANDEL

Once in a long while, a story is so bursting with charm and tenderness that its charm is irresistible. That story is Sharlie and Brian's story, *Change of Heart*— a love story for a lifetime.

A Dell Book $2.95 (11355-5)

At your local bookstore or use this handy coupon for ordering:

**The second volume in the
spectacular Heiress series**

The Cornish Heiress

by Roberta Gellis
bestselling author of
The English Heiress

Meg Devoran—by night the flame-haired smuggler, Red Meg.
Hunted and lusted after by many, she was loved by one man
alone...

Philip St. Eyre—his hunger for adventure led him on a
desperate mission into the heart of Napoleon's France.

From midnight trysts in secret smugglers' caves to wild
abandon in enemy lands, they pursued their entwined destinies
to the end—seizing ecstasy, unforgettable adventure—and
love.

A Dell Book   **$3.50**   **(11515-9)**
